Acclaim for *Kissing through a Pane of Glass*

'A touching story' *Spectator*

'The story is a moving one, skilfully told'
Financial Times

'Powerful and disturbing' *Literary Review*

'A compelling guide to romantic pain and responsibility'
She

'An impressive debut' *New Woman*

'Very readable...he writes about sex with a beguiling honest' *Time Out*

'Enchantingly written, unceasingly interesting and already one of the best books of 1993. A major find'
Tamworth Herald

Also by Peter Michael Rosenberg

Touched by a God or Something

Kissing through a Pane of Glass

Peter Michael Rosenberg

A Touchstone Book
Published by Simon & Schuster
New York London Toronto Sydney Tokyo

For Therese Campbell

Acknowledgements

With special thanks to my agent, Christopher Little, and my editor, Lucy Ferguson

---

First published in Great Britain by
Simon & Schuster Ltd, 1993
First published in Great Britain by Touchstone, 1994
An imprint of Simon & Schuster Ltd
A Paramount Communications Company

Copyright © Peter Michael Rosenberg, 1993

This book is copyright under the Berne Convention
No reproduction without permission
All rights reserved

The right of Peter Michael Rosenberg to be identified as author of this work has been asserted in accordance with sections 77 and 78 of the Copyright Designs and Patents Act 1988

Simon & Schuster Ltd
West Garden Place
Kendal Street
London W2 2AQ

Simon & Schuster of Australia Pty Ltd
Sydney

A CIP catalogue record for this book is available from the British Library

ISBN 0-671-85098-9

This book is a work of fiction. Names, characters, places and incidents are either the product of the author's imagination or are used fictitiously. Any resemblance to actual events or locales or persons, living or dead, is entirely coincidental.

Printed in Great Britain by HarperCollins*Manufacturing*, Glasgow

1

I find it easy to love. I come from a loving, demonstrative family. My father cuddled me as a child — we still greet each other with a hug and a kiss — and my mother showered me with care and affection. Words of love and comfort were scrawled across the blank pages of my early life, and like blotting paper I soaked up every inky drop, until my soul was stained blue-black permanently with the excesses of my parents' affection. I became saturated with all that touching and kissing and warmth. Is it any wonder that in my adult life I have searched for women who will wring me dry, women to whom I can give some of that excess love?

My motives have not been purely altruistic; of course not. Love is a heavy burden. If I can bring happiness into someone's life by loving them, then so much the better. But they have to want it, they have to be able to accept it, or else I remain weighed down. And I don't want to feel weighed down. I want to feel light, I want to feel good. Liana believes none of this, of course. She thinks that I have no idea what love is, and she sees this as a problem.

It isn't a problem, because it simply isn't true. But try telling Liana that.

We were sitting in the living room watching television last night – one of those film review programmes – when Liana started to fidget. I don't know but I guess I must be getting tired or careless or perhaps prematurely senile, because I *know* that when she gets that way, Something is going to Happen. There's all manner of things I can do if I catch this early enough; walking out of the room is a good one. Alternatively, I can prepare myself for the inevitable onslaught, and either parry and thrust in self-defence, or just ignore it and let myself be stabbed to pieces. I can even launch a pre-emptive strike and immobilise her before she gets into her stride. Whatever, if I'm tuned in, I can deal with it. Last night, however, I was feeling too relaxed, and I just didn't see it coming.

'Your problem,' said Liana in a manner which suggested that someone in the room had actually asked her opinion, 'is that you are pathologically incapable of distinguishing between love and sex.'

Liana loves saying "pathological", even though she doesn't know what it means. She thinks it adds credence to an otherwise meaningless statement, as if long words conferred official sanction, transforming ill-informed opinion into irrefutable fact. Now I've been hearing this accusation a fair bit lately, so I'm well aware that there's more to come, a little exposition, perhaps even a suggestion as to what action might be taken to "cure" my "problem". So I said nothing at the time and allowed

Liana to carry on with her potentially poisonous little discourse.

'The root of all your anxieties,' she continued, sitting straight-backed in a chair that was designed for lounging in, manufactured for people who like to slouch, 'is your refusal to accept the simple fact that you are over-sexed. You meet a pretty girl, she gives you the come-on, and hey-presto, you're "in love". It's not only absurd, it's pathetic. A chronic case of self-delusion.'

There she goes again. Of course, neither of us know if there is such a thing as "a chronic case of self-delusion", but this is the sort of pretentious psychobabble that Liana thinks will impress me.

It doesn't, of course. It just aggravates me. Where Liana gets these ideas from is anyone's guess.

She seemed calm enough while she was telling me all this, so it was safe to assume that there would be no tantrums, no tears. I noted that there was even the hint of a smile on her lips as she was saying all these daft things. It wasn't typical behaviour, but at least I knew it was safe.

'You're a sick man, Michael. You need professional help.'

I don't mind Liana being pretentious, offensive, even plain wrong. I've had to put up with all those things, and worse, for a long time now. But when she becomes condescending I tend to hit back.

'Liana, do me a favour. Fuck off.'

Water off a duck's back. She was in one of her indestructible modes.

'Your aggression doesn't bother me, Michael. It's just

further proof of your hatred of women. You think you love women, don't you Michael. You think you're just overflowing with love for them. But that's a lie. You hate women. All you want to do is use them, fuck them, fool them into thinking they're in love with you, and then, when you've caught them, when they've become dependent, when they've burnt their bridges, you leave them. You're a disgrace Michael. You should be locked up. You should be castrated.'

Ladies and gentlemen, meet Liana, my best friend.

'Define love,' said Liana this morning, as we sat together in the Café Flores. I cannot begin to tell you how many times Liana has asked me this same question lately. She's always been obsessed with love and all that, but this is beyond a joke. The annoying thing is, she knows how I feel. She's known for years. Liana is trying to bait me, and the only thing I don't know is why.

I ignored her question and continued stirring sugar into the thick black coffee that Julio, the owner of the café, brews to perfection. Café Flores is like a second home to me when I'm in London; I feel safe here, I can relax. It's cosy, with its red-and- white chequered table cloths, the polished wooden floors, the white net curtains, the voice of Pavarotti – just audible above the hissing and spluttering of the gleaming silver espresso machine – singing popular arias. And that wonderful coffee.

This morning my hand was shaking; the legacy of the previous night's altercation with a bottle of Scotch.

Johnny Walker and I went the full fifteen rounds. It was a close thing, and the judges were, I feel, undecided until the last few minutes. Alas, J.W. floored me in the final round; an undisputed K.O. I should have known better; it was hardly the first time. The hangover and the trembling limbs were part of the price I had to pay for being so indulgent, for having such a lousy memory. I am living proof that behaviourism is a fallacy.

'Go on, define love,' said my hectoring companion, beaming at me, bright-eyed. Something's come over Liana lately; she's become afflicted with an acute case of the "holier-than-thous". I have my suspicions. I think she may have become possessed. The Spirit of Smugness lurks uncomfortably in the air around her. It is an ugly demon.

I wanted to say all this to her and more, but I couldn't face an argument so I said nothing. And as a result, as well as not wanting the conversation to falter, Liana, ever-prescient, decided to answer for me. She's thoughtful like that.

'I'll tell you what your definition of love is. Love is when some starry-eyed bimbo with big tits and long legs says she'll let you come in her mouth . . .'

I sprayed coffee all over the table. 'Jesus, Liana. Do you have to be so gross?'

'Tell me it's not true.'

'It's not true.'

'Liar.'

See what I'm up against?

'Be honest, Michael. All you ever think about is sex.'

'Liana, it strikes me that if anyone has become obsessed with sex lately, it's you.'

Liana raised her eyebrows, too deliberately to be convincing. She gave a little sniff. She paused.

'Attack,' intoned my beloved, 'is the best form of defence.'

She was right. I wanted to punch her right on her pert little stuck-up nose.

I didn't, of course. And in case you're wondering why I'm prepared to put up with all this abuse, the answer is, I'm afraid, both simple and dreadfully predictable.

I love her.

2

I was just twenty-one when I met Liana. I had graduated from one of the "radical" new universities with a good degree in a thoroughly useless subject and, having worked during the vacations, had saved enough money for my first trip to Asia. Travelling to India was still considered something of a real adventure in those days, and I had spent most of my final year reading anything and everything about the sub-Continent in preparation for the trip. I was not only young and inexperienced, but also possessed of a rare naïveté for one who had spent three years at Sussex. I must have numbered among just a handful of students who had not experimented with soft drugs, had not defied his tutors, had not got into trouble with the police/local authorities, and had not slept around. That is, I had not slept around much. I had already completed my first year of study before I lost my virginity. In fact, it wasn't so much a loss as an exchange. Joanne, eighteen, petite, pretty and even more ingenuous than I, gave herself willingly (after three months) to me and I, claiming no more experience than she, gladly accepted. It was not, of course, as easy as I had anticipated.

Not to put too fine a point on it, I was not a particularly handsome young man. As a child, it might be said, I was downright ugly. More bluntly, improvements that one might have hoped for in adolescence had not materialised, and in my late teens I had a face that, whilst not exactly repulsive, was no competition for either Messrs Redford or Newman, at that time joint equal heart-throbs on the big screen. Diplomatically, people would say I had a characterful face, and would add — lest this seem ungracious — that I had a lovely smile.

When I met Joanne I was in the process of growing a beard for the first time in an attempt to disguise my weaker-than-average chin, and draw attention away from my larger-than-average nose. Prior to this time, I had had just one girlfriend, a shy, rather nervous girl called Diane, who screamed every time I attempted to feel her breasts or thighs. Consequently, my familiarity with the female anatomy was severely limited, restricted to the information gleaned from a few biology text books and a rather tatty copy of *Health and Efficiency*.

During that first year at Sussex I made several attempts to "have it off", but I fear my looks did not drive women crazy with desire, unlike my best friend Richard, who only had to look at women in a certain way and they'd be dropping their knickers before names even had been exchanged. I, however, had to resort to other tactics: the smooth chat-up (hopeless), the cool, uninterested observer (disastrous), even bribery (fatal). All my efforts were to no avail.

I was eighteen years old, away from home for the first time, nobody looking over my shoulder, surrounded by young, nubile, beautiful women, most of them eager to "experiment", and all I could do was wander around campus with a desperate expression and a permanent erection.

And then I grew the beard.

It worked wonders. Sporting no more than five days straggly growth, I went to yet another party, met Joanne, and fell in love. When, after three months of sleeping in the same bed, having made only the briefest and most tentative explorations of each other's bodies, we finally decided to do it, I was somewhat distressed to find the focus of my attention in such an inaccessible location. The biology books had made no mention of this. Don't get me wrong; I knew what I had to do and where I had to do it; I just hadn't expected it to be so tricky.

After three or four breathless attempts, and just before I was about to give up for good, what I later discovered was termed "intromission" was achieved. You'd have thought, from the look on my face for the next two weeks, that like some great, intrepid explorer delving into unmapped territory, I had single-handedly discovered sex.

It was the start, as they say, of something big.

Joanne remained my sole partner during the next two

years, and when we finally split up just before graduation, it was not with any great sadness. Although we were still only children, we had outgrown each other. Joanne had chosen a profession to follow, whilst I had set my sights on conquering the world, or at least, travelling all over it. Our two paths diverged at that point, and would never again cross over.

I was, therefore, unattached when I arrived in New Delhi, eager for new experience and, having not had sex for several months, horny as hell.

I arrived at Sunny's Guest House, a perfectly acceptable dive in New Delhi, booked into a room and fell into a comatose collapse for five hours. Revived thereafter by an invigorating cold shower and precarious excursion to the squat bog, I sat in the open rooftop courtyard and soon found myself deep in conversation with fellow travellers. This was what it was all about: the "where have you been, where are you going" exchanges, the shared horror stories of life on the road. I drank tea, chatted amiably, tried to remember snippets of advice as they were thrown around the rooftop like volleyballs and thought: that didn't take long; already I feel at home.

I was wrong, of course.

Two hours later, wanting to soak up a little atmosphere, I made my way to the old city. How was I to know that this was asking for trouble? Old Delhi was to be my first experience of the real Asia. Jetlagged, excited, I was not suitably prepared.

Dusk fell. I found myself walking nervously down

the claustrophobically crowded alleyways side-stepping rickshaws, goats, cows, filth, dirt and chaos, carcasses crawling with flies, rotten fruit, rancid butter, red-streaked bones on splintered wooden trestles, green parrots crammed into rusted cages. And wall-to-wall people: crying, running, screaming. Thick clouds of steam billowed into the twilight shadows, the over-powering odours of spices, meat, shit and piss suffocated me, my vision assaulted by excess, my conscience stabbed by the sight of scabrous lepers and limbless beggars. No space, no freedom, no release, a seething mass living a life of unimaginable squalor. Holding my breath, squinting against the horror, shoved from every side at every pace, I dragged myself through this insanity for three hours. Put this many Europeans together in such a space and there'd be rioting, murder. Yet in the lee of the Friday mosque it all functioned like a surrealistic ballet, each move choreo-graphed to mesh in with every other. But it was too much for me; something cracked inside and I had to get out. I began to wonder what I had let myself in for. This was not my vision of India, a vision composed of tranquil views of the Taj Mahal, majestic sightings of palaces and forts.

It was an equally terrifying journey back to New Delhi in the pitch black rush-hour on the back of an eight-seater *Tempo*, a tin can mated with an old Harley Davidson that crashed and weaved through the manic traffic, a near collision with a car, and near extinction between truck and bus. And my eyes-nose-hair full of exhaust and grime, catching in the throat, sealing the nostrils.

I was nervous. I thought, I've only just arrived and this could be my last ride.

I couldn't wait to get back to the guest house, an oasis of calm in this Sodom of a city.

It took three weeks to acclimatise to India, my feelings, throughout, ambivalent. Sometimes I would wake in the morning, wanting nothing other than to be home, away from the madness, safe and secure among family and friends. By the evening of the same day, having experienced yet another facet of that extraordinary country, I would decide that I would stay for ever.

It was in this frame of mind that I arrived in the lake city of Udaipur in the desert state of Rajasthan.

3

'Make love to me.'

'Don't be ridiculous.'

'Come on, make love to me.'

'Give me a break . . .'

'Why don't you want to make love to me? I'm pretty, aren't I? I've got big tits and long legs . . .'

'Liana, please . . .'

'I'll tell you why. I'll tell you why you won't make love to me. Because I'm not a bimbo, that's why. Because you know I'll never fall for your clever lies. Because I'll never scream your name and tell you I love you . . .'

'Leave me alone, Liana. I'm trying to work.'

'You know what your problem is, don't you Michael?'

Yes Liana, I do. My problem is you. My problem is that you have turned my life from paradise to purgatory. My problem is that I can't get rid of you. My problem is that I hate what you do, but love who you are. Or were. Which probably makes me as crazy as you.

'Don't ever say it. Don't ever tell me that you love me.'

'I wouldn't dream of it.'

'Do you understand? *Never*. If you ever say it, I'll kill you. I'll take a knife and stick it between your ribs. I'll cut your balls off. Do I make myself clear?'

'Transparently so.'

'Don't be smart with me you bastard.'

'Liana! Enough!'

'Don't shout at me! Who the fuck do you think you are? Who the *fuck* do you think you are?'

I stopped writing, pushed the chair back from the desk, turned round and ducked just in time to avoid having my face remodelled by a flying glass paperweight. The paperweight slammed into the wall behind me, but for some reason did not shatter. Liana was standing on the other side of the room, her body turned away from me, her hands shaking. She was staring intently at the floor. She bit down on her lower lip and I sat there, paralysed, knowing what would happen next. No words would help now.

She struggled to maintain control, to stop the tears, her entire body contorting in ugly spasms, as if she were indeed possessed. I saw the agony in her eyes, watched helplessly as her lower lip started to quiver, every muscle straining to keep from crying. Then all at once, her face became crumpled like a used paper bag, and an unholy, demented howl, drawn up from God-knows-where, filled the room.

I went over and put my arms around her. She didn't push me away but buried her face in the folds of my shirt, as if trying to burrow into my chest. She wept for an hour, barely making a sound, and it was all I could do to stop myself from sobbing out loud.

It's been like this for a long time now, for as long as I can remember. And I know it will never change. You'd think I'd be used to it by now. Tomorrow will be even worse. Liana knows I'll be going away soon.

No one has ever seen this side of her; our friends would be shocked if they knew the truth. They'd be horrified.

But they'll never know. Never.

It's our little secret.

Before I tell you of my first meeting with Liana, there are a few things you should know about me, or rather, about my early sex life. Nothing smutty, just a few words that might help explain my present predicament. Otherwise, nothing will make much sense.

Joanne, my first partner, was slim, about five feet two inches in height, and had a beautifully shaped body with full, firm hemispherical breasts, a neat, small waist, and a beautiful peach-like bottom. Sex with Joanne, whilst never earth-shattering, was, for the most part, highly pleasurable and full of warmth and gentle humour. We did not experiment much (what, after all, would two virgins know about experimentation?) and I suppose the most daring thing we did was eschew the mattress in favour of alternative items of furniture.

Joanne was not my idea of the perfect woman, but over a period of two years I became accustomed to making love to a woman who had what standard Western tastes would call "a good figure". During all the time that the two of us stayed together, I was never unfaithful to Jo. There were more attractive women around the University, certainly, but whilst I may have looked, I never touched. Remember, I considered myself fortunate to have a girlfriend at all, let alone one who many (myself included) considered sexy, and I did not delude myself into thinking that the stunning blondes and leggy brunettes would fall for my increasingly clever patter and straggly beard when the competition consisted of several hundred chisel-chinned, dark-eyed he-men.

However, such things do not stop a man from dreaming, and there were occasions when I would fantasise about, say, Valerie, the Jane Fonda lookalike who studied in the School of Social Sciences. Women like Valerie set my pulse racing and made me go weak and stupid. On the two occasions when I met her, I managed to make a complete idiot of myself, due, certainly, to the knowledge that *this* was the sort of woman that I wanted above and beyond all others, and – the miserable truth – that I would never have her.

Although my confidence had improved dramatically by the time I graduated, I was still not aware that I possessed something that women would later refer to as my "sexual magnetism". I still mistakenly believed that women equated "sexy" with "good-looking", and were turned on only by men with square jaws, bustling biceps, come-to-bed eyes and big bulges in their underpants. It never occurred to me (and would not for some time) that I could be desired by beautiful women. In fact, I often wondered why Jo didn't leave me; there were plenty of better looking men than me around, most of whom had shown more than just a passing interest in her, and I think she could have had her pick. I figured she stayed with me because it was safe, comfortable, and because I had been the first man she had slept with. I never thought about leaving Jo, not simply because I loved her, but because I felt certain that I could do no better.

Richard, on the other hand, had bedded more women during his three years at university than the combined conquests of the entire School of Engineering and Applied Sciences (127 mostly acned males and one hermaphrodite). Like I said, Richard had this look about him – a bit like a more rugged version of James Dean – and women seemed to go weak at the knees when he walked into the room. I was envious beyond all reason. Maybe I was mistaken and it was all in my imagination. Perhaps Richard lied about all the women he'd laid. The truth was irrelevant; I knew all too well what *I* believed at that time: Richard was proof positive that only good-looking men screwed beautiful women, and as far as I was concerned, this was an irrefutable fact of life, as certain as sunrise.

The pseudo-Fondas and Bardots paraded through my fantasy world like ghosts walking through walls, and all I could do was hope that somewhere there was a kind, benevolent God who would look down on me with pity and compassion and grant me, just once, a night with a sex-starved Venus whose only desire was to perform acts of unspeakable depravity with a horny little human being who had a big nose and no discernible chin.

4

When Venus appeared, I was wholly unprepared. In fact, I had not expected to meet anyone that day, let alone the most beautiful woman I had ever laid eyes on. I had deliberately chosen to eschew company; it was my second day in Udaipur, and I needed some quiet time alone to assimilate all that had happened to me in the three weeks since I had arrived in India.

One should be prepared for India, and in my preparations I had spoken to many people who had travelled here. But none of them had mentioned noise to me; no one had said, "Oh, by the way, about noise..." Why didn't anyone say anything? I have returned to India many times over the years, and it is always the same. I mean, we're not just talking about the background sounds of everyday life, nor are we talking intermittent bursts of rowdiness. We're talking full blast sensory assault; we're talking auditory GBH. Noise in India is as dynamic, as varied, as all pervading as anything you might set eyes upon, only whereas you can close your eyes or stare into space, you cannot stop hearing. You cannot close your ears. Not to the yelling and screaming; not to the amplified strangulations of the muezzin calling the faithful to prayer; not to the thunderclaps and gunfire bursts of motorbikes backfiring; not to the continual roar of a thousand combustion engines, each revving well past built-in tolerances. Not to the ubiquitous and continual blasts of horns, full blown symphonic sustains, all in unison if not harmony. Not to the discordant wail of Indian pop music blaring from flared horns at street corners, on trucks, wherever. Not to the dawn chorus of hawking and spitting, each de-phlegming a cacophony of bodily and guttural reverberations culminating in an expectorated crescendo.

You cannot close your ears, either, to the malevolent street traders, rickshaw drivers, store owners and "official" guides with their, "Just look, no buy", "Where you go, I take you", "Come look at my postcards" and, "I guide you, good price". And more: the rattling of ruined rotor blades and eccentric extractor fans, the gurgling of prehistoric plumbing and the slamming of rickety doors. The cries of children, the squeal of pigs . . . There is noise and there is noise, but in India, there is only the latter.

After the madness of Delhi, Udaipur came as something of a surprise to me. I was just getting used to the idea that India was a noisy, smelly, filthy, overcrowded madhouse, and suddenly this glorious city appeared, like an oasis in the desert, to confound and delight me. On my first day I wandered around awestruck, trying to absorb in its entirety all that I set my eyes upon, from the lowliest shack to the grandest edifice.

Udaipur was dominated by its wonderful City Palace, the grandest and the largest that I had seen at that time. Standing on the edge of Lake Pichola, it was a magnificent structure, an immense folly, composed of turrets and towers, cupolas and balconies, built in grand Moghul style, totally overshadowing the lake edge. The years had not been kind to the City Palace, and time had taken its toll; walls were crumbling, paint was peeling, and much of the interior had been given over to a museum housing a sad collection of inconsequential garbage, but even so, the place still reverberated with the glory of its former days.

Lying in the shadow of the palace, between the main buildings and the lake, I discovered a strange, timeless no man's land of forgotten courtyards, open stairways, empty passages and ruined walkways. In this peaceful, half-awake world lived a small community of squatters who had made their homes among the rubble and detritus. I wandered through this area with a growing fascination, taken aback by the sheer oddity of its existence. In order to make my way through this dream world, I had to traverse a convoluted, maze-like route. Every now and then I'd find myself following a passageway leading to a staircase that would in turn give on to a deserted open terrace that offered the most spectacular view of the lake and its crowning glory, the white marble fantasy of the Lake Palace, a shimmering mirage that appeared to float upon the surface of the lake.

Such was the power that this extraordinary building held on the imagination, that whenever it came into view

I would stop in my tracks and stare in awe and disbelief. At one such terrace the view was completely unobscured, so I sat down on the cool flagstones, positioned my back against the wall, and marvelled at the spectacle. The air was clear and warm, the sky a brilliant, undisturbed blue. Ahead of me, the waters of the lake rippled in the gentle breeze, and the only sounds to be heard were the occasional birdcall and the steady rhythms of wet fabric being beaten against stone, as the *dhobi wallahs* executed their clothes-washing duties.

I must have sat there, mesmerised, for a couple of hours, drawing in the visions before me, mulling peacefully over the events of the previous few days. It was the first peaceful time I had had since my arrival.

By late afternoon the sun – no longer beating down from on high – had entered my general field of view, heralding a magnificent sunset which lay just a couple of hours away. How lucky I am, I thought to myself, to have been allowed to witness this, to experience this moment.

And as if this wasn't enough to keep a twenty-one-year-old entranced, into this dream walked another, more splendid vision.

'Have you ever seen anything more beautiful?'

The interruption should have shocked me, jolted me out of my reveries, caused me, at the least, consternation. But it did not. The voice was as peaceful as the scene I had been gazing at, and I merely turned my head to discover who had spoken.

'Have you?'

I had not.

That first sight of Liana still registers as one of the few perfect moments of my life. She had walked, silently, on to the terrace, and was standing to my left. She was wearing a simple cotton dress with an Indian print design and leather sandals. She appeared tall, lithe; the sun, behind her, shone through her dress so that her figure was outlined in partial silhouette: a beautiful shape. I believe I gave an involuntary gasp, which Liana probably interpreted as surprise. She turned her head a little towards me to look across to the mountains, and I set my eyes upon the profile that would haunt me all of my days. She was possessed of a beauty unlike anything I had ever encountered before. She oozed sexuality from every pore.

The feelings, emotions and passions that pulsed through me in that moment had a character, a taste, a shape that was unique, other-worldly, ecstatic. Even in that desert heat, with the sweat running down my back in rivulets, shivers ran through my body. This was not a normal reaction, not a sensible, considered response. It was not natural. For a moment I was all but overwhelmed; fear took hold of me, gripped me around the throat like an iron hand, a vice. I did not know its nature, or why I should suddenly feel so scared, but it was as real a feeling as anything I had ever experienced. The beads of sweat that now broke out across my forehead were cold, clammy. A loud, buzzing noise inside my head made me feel sick. I closed my eyes momentarily, trying to regain control. What was this? What was wrong with me?

Try as I might, I could make no sense of what I was feeling, of what was happening to me. I opened my eyes again, drawing in the vision before me, the splendour and perfection of another human being, a woman so beautiful that the mere sight of her was capable of reducing me to a mute, quivering idiot. And then it dawned on me. Despite all my fantasies and daydreams, despite what I knew about my needs and lusts, until that moment I had never really known what true desire was, and that, in its purest form, it was a terrible and frightening thing. I did not know her name or where she had come from. All I knew – to my eternal shame thereafter – was that, whoever she was, I wanted to possess her, entirely.

5

In those days, whenever anyone asked me what I did for a living, I told them I was a travel writer. This was a lie. I had not, as yet, attempted to put pen to paper, and even on that first trip to India I had made no provision to keep a journal. History records that it was to be three years before I was to publish so much as a single article. If events from that trip have been recorded in any way, then such information resides in the convoluted spirals of my increasingly unreliable memory.

My declaration of so specific a profession was not the result of delusion or a fevered imagination, or even the wish to impress others. Nor did I consider myself a *de facto* liar. It was more a case of wish fulfilment. I *wanted* to be a travel writer and believed the swiftest route to achieving this goal was to set out with the firm belief that I was already a member of that select élite.

In retrospect, it is outrageous that I should have persisted with this falsehood, and lauded my mythical reputation with such vehemence. "You haven't heard of me? But surely . . . you do read the Sunday papers? You must have seen my name. No? No matter . . ."

And so on. I believed then that travel writing was my passport to glory, fame, independence, wealth and freedom. More fool me. But such are the dreams of the young, and, despite the fact that I had yet to consign a single descriptive scenario to paper, I felt certain of my vocation and of the glittering prizes that inevitably awaited me.

Of course at that time I did not differentiate between confidence and egoism. Indeed, if anyone dared accuse me of egocentricity, I would flare up at them, angered by the implied defamation. But this is no crime, and whilst I may regret some of my more flamboyant displays in defence of my integrity, even now I do not condemn my former self for such excesses.

Twenty-one-year-olds are entitled to be brash, optimistic, egotistical. They have, in fact, a right to such feelings. They have yet to suffer the blows of disappointment that start to rain down as one grows older; they have yet to become world-weary. We should applaud and sanction their self-belief, because as we approach that chimerical phase of life known as adulthood, with its attendant uncertainties and complications, it is our belief in ourselves and our confidence in our abilities that is most swiftly eroded, and we are left without dreams, desire and the energy required to achieve our goals. So do not be angry with twenty-one-year-old Michael Montrose and his wide-eyed naïveté, his swaggering bravado, his inability to accept even the most mild criticism. Allow him these few brief months – maybe years – of unbridled enthusiasm. You, too, were once young.

Remember?

I was to learn, eventually, that it is no easy matter trying to make a decent living as a travel writer. It sounds like a cushy number, doesn't it? One of the great glamour professions – travel the world, visit exotic locations, scribble down a few impressions and hey presto, money in the bank. What could be easier?

Trying to fly of one's own volition, that's what. Or inscribing the New Testament on the head of a pin.

The problem is, anyone who can scrawl their name on a piece of paper and has been further afield than Bognor, thinks they can write travel articles. They believe their visions and versions are as valid as the next person's, and consequently there's no reason why they shouldn't get paid for their well-informed opinions. The really sickening thing about this is, it's true. The competition is phenomenal, especially these days. Independent travel has become the Holy Grail of the late twentieth century. Anyone with a few hundred pounds and a couple of months can now become a Grand Explorer. The world is full of roving bands or neophyte reporters, searching for the exotic, having "experiences", seeking nirvana. The Third World has become an event supermarket, complete with daily specials, bargain offers and cut-price, shop-soiled goods. You just wander along the aisles selecting the desired items according to taste and cost (Thailand: convenience; most attractive packaging. India: cheapest, best value on offer. Galapagos Islands; most expensive and exclusive commodity etc.). Head for the check-out, flash the credit card and *voilà*, instant life experience (which, like instant coffee, may be more convenient and cheaper than the real thing, but bears only a passing similarity to it). And just like shopping at Tesco, you can't help but feel at the end of the day that you've been conned, seduced. You arrive home, look at what you've purchased, and what do you find? Fancy packets filled with mass-produced, processed muck which is full of artificial additives and tastes of nothing much in particular. It is also, invariably, over-priced and bad for your health.

The great travel writers know the truth. Paul Theroux, Eric Newby – they know that travelling is a dreadful experience, circumscribed by boredom, loneliness, frustration, confusion and sickness. To add insult to injury, one pays good money and expends valuable time in the process. They're honest enough to tell us all this (especially Theroux), but do we listen? We do not. We become envious of their amoebic dysentery; their sleepless nights in flea-infested hotel rooms that double up as brothels; their endless hours of aggravation at the hands of insane Customs officials who are not content with merely ripping their bags apart, but wish to do the same thing to their bodies, having first raped them at gunpoint. We remain victims of the travel agents' brochurese gobbledegook. We have been brainwashed by too many repeats of *The Holiday Programme* and *The World About Us*.

We have nothing better to do with our time. And we are all aroused by the lure of the exotic.

If you're looking for villains in this tawdry little exercise in mass deception, look no further. I am the worst offender. Unlike Theroux and Newby, I am a rotten stinking little liar, a purveyor of petty fibs and terminological inexactitudes. I rhapsodise about the beautiful peacock-blue lakes that shimmer in the heat-haze, and ignore the dead bodies floating on the surface. I eulogise about the awe-inspiring walks through the snow-capped mountain ranges and neglect to mention the sky-high piles of faeces on the paths. And I enthuse about the uniqueness, the matchless quality of the moment, forgetting, conveniently, to mention that there will be hordes of other people standing beside you, wondering what all the fuss is about. Whilst others are economical with the truth, I am deliberately mean, premeditated in my parsimony. And I do it all for money. I'm selling ersatz experiences and false dreams. I am a whore. On the integrity scale you will locate me somewhere between a used car salesman and a child molester, and if my Hindu friends in Udaipur have got it right, I shall probably return in my next life as a dung-beetle.

Or a politician, perhaps.

Maybe I shouldn't be so hard on myself. After all, I'm merely performing a necessary function, one that – had I chosen a more noble profession – would have been executed by someone else. The fact is, for all the lies and bullshit, people still want to travel. It all rather begs the question.

The late Bruce Chatwin – probably the greatest commentator of all about the process of travel – had a beautiful theory. Man, he said, is intrinsically nomadic, that it is virtually his purpose to walk, to travel, to be for ever in the act of moving on, and that the whole concept of civilisation, of stationary society, is a mistake, an error, a miscalculation.

It's a lovely idea, and I wish I could believe in it. Unfortunately, I am of a wholly different and rather more prosaic opinion. Travel is a sickness, an addiction, the curse of misfits who are incapable of finding meaning in the ordinary, the everyday. They are the malcontents. They travel, not because they want to, but because they have no choice, because there is no place for them in this world, because, for their sins, they live in a continual state of partial dissatisfaction.

They are lost souls.

And so, alas, am I. So I travel, and tell my tales and sell my lies, and because I spend six months of the year living in countries where the per capita annual income is less than the fee I receive for three thousand carefully written words, I survive.

I have no home, no car, no savings. I have nothing to give to anyone except love, and now Liana wants to take that away from me. If anyone's getting used, fucked or fooled around here, it's me, wouldn't you say?

6

'Liana,' said the girl.

It could have meant anything; for all I knew, she was talking a foreign language. I was sure she could hear my heart beating. My mouth had dried completely, and I felt short of breath; for a moment the symptoms all added up to one of those dreadful diseases I had read about, the sort of thing one is bound to catch in India just by breathing the air. I was incapable of saying anything, so I just nodded. This response, or rather lack of response, must have impressed her in a way not intended.

'You don't think that's an unusual name?'

Confused, uncertain how to reply, I merely smiled. Wasn't a liana a climbing plant, one of those things Tarzan used when he went swinging from tree to tree in the jungle? 'It's a lovely name,' I said at last.

The beautiful girl returned the smile, walked across the terrace and sat down beside me.

'Everyone always says, "Oh, what an unusual name!" Then they ask me to spell it. It's so predictable, it drives me mad.' She paused a moment, and then looked at me quizzically. 'You must be a different sort of person,' she said softly. 'I think I'm going to like you.'

If my life were a film and this event a scene, then at this point something intense and dramatic would have happened. Perhaps the camera angle would have changed to an intimate two-shot; two strangers looking into each other's eyes. Cut to a close-up as two hands reach towards each other. Fingertips touch. Cut to close-up of Liana's face, eyes sparkling, lips slightly parted. Music swells in the background. Medium shot now, as his hand tentatively strokes her golden thigh. He eases her dress up to her waist. The music increases in volume – all lush strings and heavy, persistent beats – as the camera draws back and we see the two strangers undressing each other beside the lake . . .

It was not this way. We sat side by side, staring out at the blue waters, and talked amiably about our travels. We stayed on the terrace as the sun descended behind the mountains in a blaze of red and gold.

You're disappointed, right? You think this prosaic and uninteresting. Then let me clarify, let me tell you, at least, what I saw during this time, what was running through my mind.

Externally, it's true, I was cool, calm and wise; a regular Bodhisattva, in complete control. Internally, I was in turmoil, a mass of confused emotion and restrained passion. Liana sat just a few inches away from me. She sat, like myself, with her back against the wall, then brought her knees up to her chest and clasped her hands around them. She did not look at me, but stared straight ahead, presenting me with that extraordinary profile. Her short, blonde hair took on a russet hue as the sun began to set. Her sky-blue eyes were of the most perfect clarity, and her long, fine lashes seemed spun of some fine gossamer thread.

She took off her sandals, then gathered the folds of her dress up over her knees to expose her legs to the rays of the setting sun. I caught a glimpse of skimpy white cotton underwear, which set off her even tan.

Those legs. Like everything about her, they were perfect. Not a blemish, scar or freckle. No moles, discoloured patches or birthmarks. Her thighs were perfectly smooth, with just a trace of perspiration. This was all too much for me. There was no way of hiding the erection that was straining against my shorts, and rather than draw attention to it by moving, I pretended that it wasn't there. Physically I was in extreme discomfort, but I did not so much as shift position to alleviate the situation. I just sat there. Nor did I pretend not to look at her legs, as this also would have looked too obvious. So I stared at them for a while in an amalgam of lust and admiration. In fact, I had so little choice that, had Liana commented on any of this, I would have been unable to refute charges or make amends. If Liana was disturbed by my evident voyeurism, she did not show it. Every now and then she leant forward a fraction and pulled her shoulders back as if her neck or back were stiff. Other than that, she hardly moved. But even that simple, guileless movement was enough to send me into a paroxysm. I imagined leaning across to her and running my hand along the inside of her thighs, visualised the moment when my fingertips would settle on the white cotton of her panties. I could feel the tenderness of flesh, the warm, slightly damp feel of skin, the soft curls of hair. I could imagine her lying naked on the floor, arching her back and turning her head from side to side whilst in the throes of orgasm. I could see myself on top of her, supporting my weight on my elbows, thrusting deep inside her . . .

I know there is a theory that things automatically become beautiful to us if we throw our attention at them, that the reason why something is beautiful is that it draws our attention to it. If so, then Liana was the flame and I the moth – a simile that, perhaps, was rather more accurate than I realised, considering the ultimate fate of so many moths. Every now and then I would deliberately look away from Liana and cast my attention towards the water, then the palace, then the mountains beyond, then to the setting sun, and further still to the skies. There are times in our lives when we are sensitive to the undeniable but inexplicable notions of eternity and infinity. The concepts are with us daily, but we can have no intellectual comprehension of them – great minds have been driven over the edge by even attempting such things. However, every now and then we may experience an intuitive sense of the vastness, the greatness of the universe and of ourselves and of the interconnectedness of the two. People who have experienced such things usually refer to the sensation as religious or mystic. I wouldn't wish to put a name to whatever it was I felt that afternoon, other than to say it encompassed all these things and more. It was not some ethereal, namby-pamby sensation though; it was solid, earthy, real. It seemed to affect both my body and my mind, and it was both glorious and awesome, and I did not want it to end.

What was going through Liana's mind all this time I could not say. During the hours that we sat there, right until after the sun had disappeared from sight, I managed somehow to engage in ordinary light conversation. I remember her laughing frequently, so unless she was merely being polite I assumed that my stories were amusing; but, for the life of me, I could not now tell you details of that conversation.

When twilight turned to night, we left the terrace and walked to a nearby restaurant where we drank cold beers and ate very little.

7

'Are you okay now?'

'Yes. Fine. I'm sorry, Michael.'

'Don't worry.' I kissed the top of her head, stroked her hair.

'When are you leaving?'

'You know when.'

'Tell me. Tell me again.'

'Two weeks.' I heard her give another little sniff. She hugged me closer to her.

'I don't want you to go.'

'Liana . . .'

'Don't go, Michael.'

'You know I have no choice. Let's not talk about it now. I'm not going just yet. We still have some time.'

She nodded, reluctantly, then started to cry again. It's always like this when it's time for me to go. For five months Liana curses me. She screams at me, shouts at me, abuses me. Sometimes it all gets too much for her, and she'll flail away at my head and chest with clenched fists. She'll wake me in the middle of the night and accuse me of some heinous, trumped-up crime, and refuse to let me sleep until I admit my guilt. Once every three months she'll grab a kitchen knife and lock herself in the bathroom and threaten to slash her wrists.

In the final month, before it's time for me to leave, she becomes more aggressive still. She starts in on my "problem", brings up incidents from the past – both real and imagined – and accuses me incessantly of infidelity. The fits become more frequent. She talks about how she wants to see me dead, would like to kill me. And then, in the final two weeks, she becomes contrite. Soon she will start begging me to stay.

I can cope with the rest of it; the death wishes, the suicide threats, the hammering fists, the uncontrollable rage. But when she starts to beg, when she literally goes down on her knees, prostrates herself before me, grabs hold of my ankles, promises anything, everything, that's when I go to pieces.

The rest of the time when Liana isn't being crazy, she's as normal, as controlled, as relaxed as any person could be. Our friends adore her; they always have done. Liana is wonderful company; witty, charming, warm. Every man who has met Liana at these times falls in love with her. I am the focus of the most extreme envy. There's Michael Montrose, they say; he has no proper job, no home, no money. He has a big nose, a weak chin, a straggly beard, and he's married to the most beautiful woman in the world, a woman who is so evidently crazy about him that she's prepared to let him wander off around the globe for half the year. That Michael is prepared to leave such a ravishing creature is proof, they say, of only one thing.

He must be mad.

If, as some people claim, we are what we eat, then I invite you to taste a slice of my life, and savour its bittersweet irony.

There is really only one reason why I must leave Liana behind. Money. As I have already mentioned, it is not easy making a living as a travel writer. It has taken me the best part of eight years to get to this stage, and frankly, for most of that time I have had to struggle to make ends meet. Even now I make less money than most of my contemporaries. I don't like to harp on about it, after all, it was my choice; I chose to go into a profession that pays peanuts, and what's more, pays them in arrears. Currently I write for six magazines. Whilst officially freelance, I have a sort of implied contract with the editors of four of these magazines, each of whom agree to publish between ten and twelve of my articles a year. The other two will publish occasional pieces, only these articles must be accompanied by photographs or illustrations. None of these agreements are in writing; should any or all of them suddenly decide that they no longer require my pieces, I am – to use the vernacular – well and truly fucked.

Anyone who has ever had any dealings with the publishing world will know that as soon as one enters the waters they turn from warm, inviting pools into shark-infested seas. Or worse, murky, polluted cesspits, which are impervious to light and smell very unpleasant. Remuneration is usually the stumbling block; payment is not made until after publication. Officially, the time period is one month. In practice, it is anything from a few days to a year. As the time between acceptance of the article and its appearance on the shelves of your local newsagent may be of the same order, it can sometimes be as long as two years between when an article is completed and when the cheque floats through the letter box to land on the carpet with an anti-climactic slap. To compound these problems, I am hopeless at keeping track of my financial affairs. All I know is that, at present, having paid the final month's rent on the flat and bought my open return ticket to Indonesia, I am broke. Somewhere, in the ethereal twilight zone that exists between several magazine accounting departments and my bank account, there floats two or three thousand pounds that may one day find their way from the former to the latter, or as I see it, from the sublime to the ridiculous.

In the meantime, I cannot count on that money. To all intents and purposes, it exists only in my imagination. Consequently I must seek yet another appointment with Mister Horace Leach, my friendly, anal-retentive bank manager, and make – what Mr Bloodsucker likes to call – "suitable financial arrangements". He already owns documents, appended with my signature, entitling him to possession of one arm and both legs in the event of my defaulting on payment, and as I have only one good limb left as collateral, securing a loan this time may well prove difficult.

Once again, Mr Leach will urge me to get into something "with greater stability"; after all, as he delights in pointing out, I'm not a "youngster" any more (this from a man who was born middle-aged) and I do have commitments. There is no point my arguing with Leach; there is no way I could make him understand the set of circumstances that have conspired against me to bring me to my present position. Leach thinks that if you're a writer, you can write anything. Why don't I write for television, he says; there must be good money in that? Sure, I want to say; TV is crying out for travel articles; perhaps we could work my last piece on Cairo into next week's *Coronation Street*? Of course, I don't say this, or anything like it. I do not wish to offend Mr Horace Leach, because if I'm lucky, Mr Horace Leach is going to give me some of his precious, middle-class, greatly stable money. So I tell him that I am in the process of doing whatever it is he suggested last time I came a-grovelling: writing Mills & Boon romances, sitcoms, radio plays, television advertisements, backs of cornflake packets.

Yes, it's demeaning, but I have no choice. I need cash to live on, money for Liana's fare back to Devon, and must arrange standing order payments to The Sanctuary for the next six months.

At least I won't have to worry about Liana; she'll be safe at The Sanctuary, probably safer than I. She will not run the risks of viral infection, malaria, sunstroke and dehydration. She will not have to deal with filthy sheets, diseased water and transport systems that cannot guarantee to get you from A to B without damage to body and/or soul. Mind you, I no longer take the sort of risks that circumscribed my travels five years ago. I don't dare. After all, if anything were to happen to me, who would take care of Liana? No, I cannot risk anything any more; I must be there for her. I must earn money to keep her safe and sound. It is my duty, my purpose, my *raison d'être*.

Welcome, folks, to the exciting world of travel writing.

8

I walked Liana back to her guest house. She was staying just a few hundred yards away from my hotel, on a narrow alleyway leading down to the ghats. She had, she said, a balcony; we could sit for a while, if I wanted to.

Throughout the evening I had been wondering what would happen when it finally came time to say goodnight. I had decided early on that I could not invite her back to my hotel room, as this would seem a blatant, transparent move. I did not dare risk failure or rejection so soon after meeting her. I knew I was powerless beside this woman and that if anything was to happen it would be at her instigation, a situation that (bearing in mind my theories concerning sexual attraction and personal appearance) seemed so unlikely as to be laughable.

And yet, she had enjoyed my company. We had sat in the restaurant for several hours, enjoying the refreshing beers, talking about our respective lives. Liana had recently graduated from the University of Kent with a degree in Fine Art. Painting was her great love, she said, but thought it unlikely she would ever make a living from her work. For the time being, however, she didn't worry about such things. It was more important for her to travel, to see some of the world, to experience something other than the insular worlds of university life and Surrey suburbia. She had felt stifled, she said; she needed freedom, a chance to be herself. She wanted to take risks; what was life without a little gamble now and then?

When she asked what I intended to do, I hesitated before answering. I had already told a dozen people that I was a travel writer, and had become so used to the idea that I almost believed it was true. But somehow, I could not look Liana in the eyes and tell her what was nothing better than a lie. She had this soulful, searching gaze which invited only honest exchanges. So I told her, quite simply, that I wanted to be a writer.

It was probably the only time I have been completely truthful in my entire life.

When Liana asked if I'd like to sit with her on her balcony, I did not dare to think it was a prelude to anything more than a final night-time conversation. We walked up the narrow staircase that led to her room, and then out on to the balcony. The balcony – just big enough for two cane chairs – overlooked the lake. It was a cool night with just the hint of a breeze coming off the lake. In the centre of the waters, the Lake Palace, outlined by a hundred flickering lamps, floated majestically whilst in the distance the easily identifiable shapes of the mountains provided a perfect backdrop.

We sat for some time in silence, just absorbing the stillness, the sense of the exotic that seemed to hang in the air like a rare perfume. The sky, crystal clear, crackled with the brilliance of a million points of light. We stared into the heavens and tried to identify the constellations, and having exhausted the ones we knew, searched for new patterns and devised names of our own. Every now and then I would look across at Liana and marvel at her beauty. By starlight her loveliness was further enhanced, and she took on an almost mystic aura, as if she were not of this world at all. Once or twice she caught me staring at her and smiled. She seemed not the least embarrassed by my attentions. I presumed that she was used to such things; one cannot be blessed with such allure and expect to pass through the world unnoticed. At some point during all of this, a shooting star scored its silver track across the skies, and Liana reached across and touched my arm.

'Did you?' she asked, her tone excited, expectant. I stared at her blankly. 'Make a wish?' she added.

'Yes,' I lied. I had barely noticed the star, preoccupied instead with the gentle touch of Liana's fingers on my arm. Suddenly I longed to see another shooting star, so that I could have a second chance. I would wish only one thing: to have this woman invite me to her bed. I would sacrifice anything, offer anything, just for one night with her. I made swift, rash promises to a God I had previously addressed only rarely. I bargained away years of my life. I promised never to ask for anything again. For one night – one hour even – of total passion and pleasure, I would even give away any right I might otherwise have to be happy in the future. Grant me, I prayed, this single wish.

These days, when people ask me if I have a faith, if I believe in God, I say yes. If they question my reasons, I tell them I have proof; personal, irrefutable proof. What sort of God do I believe in, they ask. Is he cruel? Benevolent? Omnipotent?

No, I say. None of these things. He is honest, fair and, like most people I know, neither gives nor expects to receive something for nothing. He keeps his word.

He gave me what I wanted, what I asked for. He gave me my one hour, and in return – although I did not realise it at the time – I relinquished all further claims on him, including any right I might previously have had to a happy future.

9

Richard had a theory about what constituted good sex. Good sex, said Richard – corrupting a well-known aphorism concerning creativity – was ninety per cent anticipation and ten per cent inspiration. The secret was always to maintain a sense of the unexpected. Sex became dull, he reckoned, because people fell into bad habits, became lazy and predictable. There were two ways of avoiding this unfortunate state of affairs. One: change partners regularly (as easy for Richard to do as to say) or two: use a little imagination.

The key to success was confidence. You could do anything you wanted, anything you desired, as long as you exuded a sense of knowingness. Most women, said Richard, felt inadequate in bed. Especially, he confided, the pretty ones. Women want to believe that they are free spirits, capable of engaging in all and any activities. They do not want to appear inhibited, as this suggests "problems", neither do they want to appear either naïve or unskilled. Consequently, one should never be hesitant or uncertain. Be precise but not unduly serious. Take control of the situation. Keep them guessing as this increases the excitement. Be positive and encouraging, and under these circumstances, a woman will do anything for you. *Anything*.

Richard made it all sound so easy. And perhaps, for him, it was. For the rest of us mere mortals, when it came to the pleasures of the flesh, a variation of catch-22 seemed to operate. How could you be confident until you'd had some experience, and how were you to increase your experience unless you were confident? When Jo and I made love, it was easy (once we got the hang of it). Neither of us had any expectations, nor could we make comparisons (favourable or otherwise) with anyone else. In a word, it was safe.

However, as soon as one finds oneself in bed with someone new, a different set of rules comes into play, and the questions, *those* questions, start popping up in rapid succession. Will I be any good? Will she be satisfied? How do I compare with her previous lover? How do I know what she'll like? If we try straight sex, will she think me boring and pedestrian? If I attempt anything else, will she think me a pervert? Should I play rough or be gentle?

What about oral sex?

Even for those with a little experience behind them, these questions interlace to form a net suitable for trapping even the most confident of people. To someone like myself, they constituted nothing short of purgatory. The fact is, back in those early days, *I simply did not know the answers*.

That night in Udaipur I was, therefore, confronted

with my first paradoxical feelings about sex. I wanted Liana with a desire and desperation that I had never previously thought possible. I wanted *nothing* other than to go to bed with her.

And I was scared shitless at the prospect that it might, just might, happen.

To compound the problem, as must now be evident, Liana was no ordinary woman. She made the Valeries and other film-star doppelgangers from my university days look like ugly ducklings. What was I doing even talking to this woman, never mind sitting alone with her on the balcony of her hotel room? What did I honestly think I was up to? Was I mad?

And a further problem. I had known this woman only a few hours, and already I had lied. Not to her; to myself. In my pact with God, I had asked for just one night. But I knew that, even if it were to happen, even if my wish were granted, it would not be enough. If the night was a disaster (and I had heard enough tales of such things to know that it was not an unlikely event) then I would be compelled to try again until I got it right, to prove to her that I was a great lover, a warm, wonderful human being, capable of bringing untold pleasures into someone else's existence. Someone to spend a life with.

And if it was a success, then of course I would not be able to live the rest of my life without her.

These thoughts flashed through my head in just a few seconds, in the time it takes to walk ten feet, from a balcony overlooking a lake, to a bed in a darkened room. In those few moments I discovered something about myself that I had never before suspected. Far from being a normal, well-balanced young man, in charge of my feelings, my desires, my destiny, I was a cork on the ocean, a leaf in the breeze, totally at the mercy of factors completely outside my control. Yes, I would make the decision, but I did not have the choice. The revelation, when it arrived, was both shocking and oddly reassuring: I was possessed by a demon, and the demon's name was obsession.

10

'Michael, there's something you should know.'

Liana bent over the mattress and lit a candle on the bedside table. I stood motionless, my heart in my mouth, watching her perform this simple task with easy grace. Every movement she made was tinged with the erotic; whether this was deliberate, or merely my interpretation of what was, in truth, nothing but her natural ways, I could not say.

She stood and faced me, then, grabbing the hem of her dress, pulled it up over her head and discarded the dress to one side.

'I've never done this before,' she murmured. She was bare, save for those white cotton panties. Her breasts, like the rest of her, were perfect; smooth and rounded. One instinctively wished to reach across and touch them, not in any sexual way necessarily, but just to connect with the beauty, to discover if such perfection could be real.

'I've never made love before,' she said, aware that I had not understood. 'But I want you. I want you to be the first.'

She moved forward, knelt down in front of me, and taking hold of my left ankle, took off my sandal. She must have felt me trembling, but said nothing. I looked down at her; her head was lowered, and the candlelight was reflecting off her shiny blonde hair. I could feel her breath, warm and heavy, against my legs. I lifted my right foot so that she could remove the other sandal. I didn't dare touch her; I could not. It was as if I were the victim of a temporary paralysis. She remained kneeling, put her hands to my waist, unzipped my shorts and pulled them down. I stepped out of them clumsily, aware only of the fact that Liana's face was just inches away from the absurd sight of my erection trying to tear through the front of my underpants. She did not move but placed her hands on my thighs. Still quivering, I slipped my shirt off over my head and threw it to one side, then placed my hands gently on her shoulders. Her hands started to caress my thighs. The pressure on my penis was excruciating, and all I wanted was for her to take off my pants, to ease the discomfort. She looked up at me, registered the expression on my face which, part agony, part ecstasy, must have confused her, and then, with a careful manoeuvre, released me from my elasticated prison. The touch of her hand was heavenly, and I closed my eyes for an instant, savouring the moment.

I was, by now, so aroused that I knew if I did not do something soon, it would all be over. I stepped back a few inches, took Liana's hands and brought her to her feet. I put my arms around her, pulled her close and kissed her gently. Her body was so warm, so smooth against mine; it seemed to lock into place. Liana did not prolong the kiss but pulled back. I felt her reaching for my groin, and in a swift motion that took me completely by surprise, she sank to her knees again and kissed me on the stomach, then ran her tongue along the underside of my penis. I recall feeling a little faint, a little unsteady. She turned, stood, walked over to the bed, removed her panties, slunk on to the mattress, raised one knee, then held out her hands to me.

'Make love to me Michael,' she whispered. 'I'm yours for the night.'

When I entered Liana that first time, there was no resistance, no discomfort. It was almost as if our two bodies had been designed exclusively for this act, for each other. Liana raised her legs up, and I slipped into her so fully, so deeply, that my head swam. Every movement, every motion was charged with an intense determinism, as if there could be nothing else at that moment, no other way. I had never felt such pleasure – my whole body resonated with a deep, vibrant shudder. Liana let out a short, breathy gasp, dug her fingers into my backside, and tried to pull me in even further. With each motion, to and fro, her gasps became louder, more urgent. She looked as if she were in some sort of possessed state, transported by the rapture. I thrust harder, fighting to hold back the climax that I knew was just moments away. Every sense became heightened; her odours overwhelmed me; her body seemed to glow with the molten heat of passion. She started to buck, her back arched – just as I had envisioned it that afternoon on the terrace overlooking the lake. She drew blood from my buttocks. She screamed my name.

When I came, a moment later, bright flashes of light erupted behind my eyelids; my body contracted in frenzied spasms, and my head felt like it might explode in a single, symphonic burst. Every nerve had been sensitised, and I could barely stand the intensity of the feelings. For a moment I thought I might pass out.

My God had kept his promise. I experienced euphoria – a sensation that I had not believed really existed – for the first time in my life. I burst into tears. Liana, her face flushed, her breathing heavy, whimpered like a child. We were saturated with sweat, exhausted beyond anything I had ever experienced. I could barely move; I felt empty, devoid of all energy and emotion. Everything that I was, everything that made me a person, an individual, a human being, had been channelled into a single act of lovemaking, and I almost wished that I might die, there and then, as I knew I had reached the pinnacle of human joy and pleasure, and that nothing could ever surpass it.

A moment later I realised that I was still crying and suddenly became worried that Liana might mistake my tears of joy for sadness. In an effort to assure her that everything was okay – and as I withdrew from her – I brought my hand close to her face, intending to stroke her cheek.

And that was when the bright shining beacon of my ecstasy was extinguished for ever like a spluttering candle flame in the rain. Liana saw my hand just inches from her cheek and flinched. Her expression turned to one of terror, a convulsion of fear and pain.

'Don't hit me!' she screamed. 'Please, Michael, don't hit me!'

11

During the final chapters of my relationship with Joanne, when it came to making love, Jo expressed an increasing desire to be taken from behind. It was a position we both enjoyed, and I did not question either motive or reason. I found the sight of Jo's rump, raised and inviting, extremely erotic. It was, in practical terms, a very comfortable position, as I could thrust more deeply into her this way. I never asked Jo why she found it so exciting; it didn't seem to matter. Her response was sufficient testimony to her enjoyment.

Until one day, when it dawned on me that perhaps Jo enjoyed sex *a posteriori* because it meant that she didn't have to see my face, she didn't have to look at me. In other words, she could imagine that it was someone else making love to her, not me at all.

For a long time I dismissed these thoughts; Jo and I were in love, we were happy, we had a good, healthy sex life; why should she want to imagine someone else making love to her? After all, I never replaced Jo's face or body with someone else's, even when I closed my eyes.

No, it could not be that. The reason for her enjoyment was simple; it was different, it made a change from the other positions.

But why was it *so* exciting for her?

Try as I might to ignore it, the thoughts began to play on my mind more and more. Jo was thinking of someone else; perhaps not a mythical figure at all, but someone she knew, someone from university. I found myself getting upset by this idea, then, slowly but surely, found distress turning to anger. If Jo suggested the "exciting" position (as she had begun to refer to it) when we went to bed, my hackles would rise. I would oblige, however, but my anger would manifest itself in the act of lovemaking. I would take her roughly, aggressively. I would thrust too hard, too fast, almost as if I wanted to hurt her. At first Jo seemed oblivious to this anger. In fact, if anything, she seemed to find it even more exciting, further confirming my theory that, with me acting out of character, she could imagine even more clearly that someone else was making it with her. The vicious circle enlarged. I began to behave in odd, unpleasant ways. I would make love to Jo in this fashion and, holding back my own climax, wait until she approached orgasm, then distract her with petty, unpleasant moves. I would pull her hair, pinch her breasts, scratch her thighs. It was despicable, and I hated myself for it. But I could not help myself. On the fourth occasion when I had used these distraction techniques, I went too far. Jo was just reaching her peak when I dug my nails into the insides of her thighs, and she cried out in pain, pulled herself away from me and started to cry.

'What's the matter with you?' she cried. 'What have I done?'

Embarrassed, I feigned ignorance. 'What do you mean?'

'Oh Michael, don't do this to me! Tell me what I've done!' She was sobbing pathetically, but still I held my ground.

'Really, Jo, I don't know what you're talking about.'

'You *hurt* me.'

I blushed. 'Oh honey, I'm sorry,' I said. 'I didn't mean it,' I lied. I should have been struck down.

I held out my hands to her. 'Come here. Please, love, I'm sorry. I must have got carried away. Here, let me kiss it better.'

Jo moved, reluctantly, towards me. I could see the blue-black bruises already forming, scored with red fingernail marks, the damning evidence of my cruelty. I felt sick.

I stroked her hair, I cuddled her and tried to comfort her. I apologised again and again. I promised her I would be more careful, that I would never do it again.

I kept my word. I never did hurt Jo again. We abandoned the position, and with it desire seemed to fade. Before long, all the pleasure and excitement had disappeared completely.

Two weeks later, we said goodbye for the final time.

12

Liana turned away, buried her face in her hands and started to cry.

Some people manage to live their entire lives secure in the knowledge that the world behaves in a certain prescribed fashion, that there are rules and regulations, that everything has a set pattern. These people may occasionally be surprised, but they are never shocked. Even when they see a news report that ten thousand people have been killed in an earthquake in some remote Latin American country, and they tut-tut and say, "Shocking", even then they are not really shocked. They know about earthquakes, they know about Third World countries, they know that these things happen. They are not shocked; if anything, they are grateful, grateful that it didn't happen here. But that too is the way their world works; earthquakes happen in remote Latin American countries, not in downtown Surbiton or Purley. The sun rises in the east, leaves fall off the trees in autumn, the price of cigarettes always goes up after the Budget – this is their world – they have no concept of shock, no knowledge of what it is like to have their world give up any pretence of familiarity; for the earth to give way beneath their feet, metaphorically or literally; for the rules to stop applying; they've never suffered emotional earthquakes.

Lucky bastards.

Liana was crying; not just crying, but sobbing, and I was scared. Not just scared; I was terrified. I did not know what to do. Suddenly I felt like a small, pathetic child; I wished there were someone I could turn to for advice. But there was no one. I was all alone, six thousand miles from home, in bed with a complete stranger, and I was completely helpless. I had no idea what had brought on this outburst and even less idea of what I should do to console her. How she could have imagined that I might hit her was beyond me, but such was the fear in her eyes that I did not dare touch her lest she interpret this as a further threat. I lay there for several minutes, totally baffled, motionless, whilst the beautiful creature who had been my path to ecstasy sobbed like a hurt child.

This wasn't what I'd expected, this wasn't how it was supposed to be, *this wasn't in the rules*. My heart was beating too fast, my palms were wet, my brow cold and clammy, my mouth dry; reactions that were not so dissimilar to the rush of lust I had experienced earlier that day when I had first laid eyes on her, only now these feelings were not of delight but of fear. My overriding response was that of an unhappy little boy; I didn't *want* this, I didn't I didn't I didn't . . .

I don't know how much time passed before I eventually summoned up enough courage to whisper her name. It may have been minutes, it may have been as long as an hour. Either way she did not respond but her sobbing had abated, so very gently I placed my hand on her arm. She gave a small shudder but did not pull away. I left my hand there, applying only the merest hint of pressure, hoping this might comfort her. She said nothing; the occasional sniffs and swallowing noises were the only indications that she was awake, even alive. What else could I do? I was still so scared; what if she suddenly became completely crazy, started flailing at me with fists, broken glass, anything she could get her hands on? You think I was over-reacting? Why? I didn't know the first thing about her. The rules and regulations had been abandoned; I was floating, drifting. I was in shock.

For an hour we maintained this position, until I felt sure Liana was on the edge of sleep. I collected a sheet from the floor and pulled it up over us. Shortly, I could hear the deep regular breathing patterns of sleep.

I watched Liana the whole night. I did not move. I kept guard, a silent, lonely vigil. When night broke and the first light brought stirrings of life to the lake city, I was still awake. At about eight o'clock, Liana opened her eyes and yawned. She shifted around, looked into my eyes and smiled. She reached out to me and kissed me warmly on the lips.

'Mmmm,' she hummed. 'What a wonderful way to greet the day.' Her expression was untroubled, her demeanour calm. She snuggled up close to me, kissed my neck a few times, then found my hand and brought it between her thighs. The intimacy of the gesture and the moist warmth beneath my fingertips had me aroused in a moment. Liana stroked me and smiled.

'Well well,' she said, the trace of a giggle in her voice. 'And a very good morning to you, too.'

There was a gentle passion to our lovemaking that morning, a cooler fire, whose flames crackled and licked around us for several hours, during which time Liana showed not a hint of terror or fear, or gave any intimation of what had happened the previous night. She was, once again, the calm serene beauty who had walked into my life the previous day and set my whole world on fire. Once again I felt those strange, unique sensations. I gazed at her and every ounce of my being ached with desire. I dismissed the night's outburst without further thought. It was nothing. I had to believe this. I responded to her as if nothing had happened, as if it had been a mirage, a dream, an episode from someone else's life, not mine. Just a little misunderstanding; just a mistake.

By midday exhaustion had overtaken me, and I collapsed back on to the mattress, no longer able to fight sleep. I did not know it then, but I was in serious trouble. I had discovered, or so I believed, the true meaning of love. I was in love, hopelessly, helplessly, and it was the warmest, most exciting, most glorious of feelings. I had tasted freedom, and now I was king of the world, emperor of the cosmos. I had enticed, aroused, possessed the most beautiful woman in the world. She had wanted me, she had taken me, she had loved me. And I had been the first. There could not, I thought, be a happier being on earth. And this was only the beginning.

But it was not the beginning, at least, not the beginning of the brave new world that I imagined lay before me. It was already the end. I had, unwittingly, built a cage out of my desire, locked myself inside, and thrown away the key. I was trapped, restrained, a victim of my own passions, and I was too young to understand that I had just sentenced myself to a lifetime's imprisonment.

13

Richard once gave me a lecture on the subject of love. His opinions were straightforward, unequivocal and concise.

'There's no such thing,' said Richard.

Love was a construction, a mirage, a figment; it was a false emotion. Only people who were insecure, frightened of being alone, felt love. When people say to each other, "I love you", all they're saying is, "You take away my feelings of isolation, my aloneness, and that makes me feel safe". It was all bullshit, said Richard. No one can take those feelings away, and to put that sort of responsibility on to someone else's shoulders was not only foolish but dangerous. No one can make you feel safe, said Richard, it was all just an illusion. Face facts. You're alone. No one can see inside your head, no one can see through your eyes, no one can share your thoughts. You are a self-contained, hermetically sealed package, and the best thing anyone can do is admit that to themselves and get on with living. Most importantly, if you start bringing all that love nonsense into the bedroom, all you'll succeed in doing is screwing up one of the few genuine pleasures left to human beings. Sex was both necessary and fun; like eating and drinking, you should do it often, change the menu frequently, and always be a little hungry before you start. Don't discuss the ingredients afterwards, and don't complain about the cost or the service; if you're not enjoying it, eat somewhere else.

I could not help but be full of admiration for Richard and his approach. It was so uncomplicated, hedonistic, easy, and I don't suppose he would have cared the least bit if I'd told him that his ideas were all well and good, but that he'd never be a poet.

14

Liana and I stayed in Udaipur for a further week. On the second day I left my hotel and moved in with her. We took a double room which also had a balcony and spent every afternoon and most of each night making love. I had expected the hotel owner to express disapproval of us – we exercised little discretion – but he merely smiled whenever he saw us, a mischievous grin which, if anything, sanctioned our liaison.

For the first two days, we left the bedroom only to perform necessary functions like washing and eating. Our evenings were spent at the rooftop restaurant where we had dined on that first, fateful evening. We would sit close together, holding hands. Our hours and days were marked with a seemingly endless flow of fun and laughter. We revelled in each other. It was not just in bed that we communicated so completely. We would happily talk for hours about our lives, our worlds, travelling, philosophy, art, creativity. We rarely spoke of love. There seemed no need; words were a poor medium for expressing something that coursed through every vein, saturated every cell, electrified our spirits.

For the time being, I was happy. The memory of Liana's outburst faded but did not disappear, and if I was self-conscious in any way, it was only with regard to my movements; that is, I avoided making any swift motions of my hands or arms. If, as was often the case, I wished to stroke Liana's cheek, I would usually place my hand first upon her shoulder and slide my fingers gently upwards to meet her face. In time this became an habitual movement rather than a conscious one, its origins soon obscured.

We returned often to the terrace overlooking the lake where we had first met; sometimes Liana would bring her notebook and make sketches of the surroundings, although she would never let me look at them. I questioned her about this and she said that, being a perfectionist, she didn't like to exhibit incomplete work, and that sketches were by definition unfinished. Even though I longed to see her drawings, I didn't push her on this; although I had yet to write anything of any value, I felt sure I'd feel much the same about my own work, unwilling to let anyone read it until it was complete, polished, ready for publication.

On those occasions, whilst Liana sketched, I would simply sit and look at her. I would watch her intently, as if I could not be worthy of her until I was able to hold the whole of her in my mind, every square inch of skin, every hair, every pore. I examined her movements, the way she held her pencil, the manner in which she glanced at her watch or looked up for just a moment with the hint of a smile. I studied her breath, the way she shrugged, the flickering of her perfect eyelashes; I took stock of every action, memorised it, stored it away. If it would ever be necessary to reconstruct Liana from scratch, I held entire blueprints in my head. I did not write any of these impressions down; it was essential that it was all committed to memory. I wanted to have instant access to her, day or night, in my waking life and in my dreams, whether she was sitting beside me or a thousand miles away. I wanted to ensure that she would be with me always, that I could always relish that extraordinary beauty, that I need only close my eyes to visualise that exquisite loveliness. Liana didn't seem to mind me staring at her; she never said anything about it, accepting my behaviour as normal. Consequently I did not feel self-conscious about it. I was as happy looking at Liana as I was making love to her. Sometimes I could hardly believe that such a wondrous beauty as she was sleeping with me, Michael Montrose.

Making love lost not an ounce of fervour, not a wisp of passion; each time was as steamy, as exhilarating, as totally exhausting as the last. After each occasion I felt certain my heart would scream "enough!" and stop beating in protest at the punishment I was putting it through. Our lovemaking was the perfect amalgam of love and lust, of tough and gentle, a wondrous blend of the expected and unexpected. We seemed to guide each other through some extraordinary moves, and I found myself performing acts that I had not thought myself capable of, going beyond normal limits, reaching for greater ecstasies.

On our last night in Udaipur, as we lay in bed together after a particularly frenetic session, Liana turned to me and began running her fingers through my straggly beard.

'What do you look like without this, I wonder?' she said in a half-mocking tone.

I smiled. 'Like an accountant,' I said. 'Like a bank clerk.'

Liana laughed. 'What do you mean?'

'The original chinless wonder. You wouldn't have given me a second look.'

'Don't be daft.'

'It's true. Before I grew this beard, the exquisite combination of nose and chin was guaranteed to have pretty girls running for the hills.'

'I don't know what you're talking about. You're very handsome; you have a lovely nose.'

It was my turn to laugh. 'It's very sweet of you to say so.'

Liana's expression changed. She looked bemused; half quizzical, half offended. 'You think I'm lying to you.'

'No, no . . . it's just, well, I *know* I'm not a good-looking bloke . . .'

'You're crazy,' she said. 'You're completely crazy.'

'What?'

Liana shifted her position until she was looking down on me. She placed her hands on either side of my face, and held me firmly so that I would have had to struggle if I'd wanted to move. 'You're the most attractive man I've ever met, Michael. *The* most. You're more than handsome. You're beautiful.'

I was quite taken aback by her vehemence. No one had ever referred to my looks as handsome. No one had ever called me beautiful. And the strangest thing was, these were not just lover's words, designed to please. Liana was deadly earnest. She believed I was beautiful. I could have cried.

The noose tightened. The water rose another inch. I was a hanged man, a drowning man, and I did not even know it.

15

Liana slept most of the day today, while I tried to complete a piece about Chitwan National Park in Nepal. It's the final article in a series on the Himalayan kingdom, and it's causing me all sorts of difficulties. That's the trouble with writing a series of articles on just one country; by the time you've written twelve thousand words, you've run out of suitably appealing adjectives and original descriptive scenarios. There is only so much you can say about mountains, blue skies, medieval Asian architecture and wizened old men with faces like decaying boot leather. Thankfully with Chitwan there's the jungle to provide the setting and the animals to furnish the action. Still, my heart's not really in it, and I wish I hadn't promised the editor that I'd have it finished by the weekend. I'm sure he doesn't intend using it for at least another three months, but I daren't renege at this stage. My reputation is shaky enough as it is, and besides I need the money (even if I won't see it for an eternity).

Liana's exhausted. She didn't sleep well. Late last night she suffered another panic attack, and I was up until four this morning trying to calm her down. She gets so scared at the thought of me leaving, and her anxiety is heartbreaking. I have to remind myself constantly that, within a week of my departure, she will have forgotten all about me. The staff at The Sanctuary will attend to all her needs. She'll have a comfortable room with her own television, she'll have three decent meals a day, and she'll never be short of company as there are at least a dozen other loonies wandering around the place.

Don't give me that look. I know I shouldn't say such things, but you have no right to criticise me. You don't know what it's like. This is my way of dealing with it, my way of coping with the sad truth: my wife is a loony, a crazy, a madwoman, a paranoid schizophrenic, a manic depressive; she has lost her marbles, she is no longer playing with a full deck, she is fucked in the head. As opposed to her loving husband who is merely fucked, period.

I no longer wake up in the mornings thinking it's all been a bad dream. My life is a hollow, pathetic thing. If, as sometimes occurs, I suffer the agonies of a nightmare, when I wake it is not to relief, but to greater anguish. For my reality is worse than the most frightening of dreams.

I look not for pity or understanding; just, perhaps, acceptance. I hold no one responsible, I harbour no resentment, least of all towards Liana. I have brought all this on myself.

Richard would never have understood. Nobody *has* to do anything, he would say. You're a free man, a free spirit, restricted only by society's conditioning and imposed moralities. If you want to kill somebody, you can do it. You make the decision, you pay the price, but you're *free* to do whatever you want. Richard loved *Crime and Punishment* but thought Raskolnikov was a jerk for making such a song and dance about his own guilt. Guilt was another of Richard's pet hates. Like love it was another figment. It all came down to insecurity; be certain of your actions and you need never feel guilty. Richard couldn't stand ambivalence, procrastination, indecision or bleeding-heart liberalism. He'd have made a great fascist. "Personal choice, Michael; that's all there is."

Perhaps he was right. Perhaps our views were not so far removed from each other. If you come to a fork in the road where the left-hand path leads to freedom and the right to incarceration, and, having chosen (for whatever reason) the latter path, you are then forced by someone to take the former, just how free does that make you? Personal choice, Richard? There are some concepts that Richard will never understand, like the idea that there exist things beyond mere self-interest. Richard's path may well lead to freedom, but it would be a lonely, isolated sort of place. When he arrives, he may well be shocked to discover that he is the only person for miles around.

When I stood at the fork in the road, Richard, I was free to make my choice. The path to the left – your route – was open, spacious and silent. To the right the way was dark, narrow, claustrophobic, and away in the distance a sad, troubled beautiful voice called my name . . .

16

We sat on the lawn of the Pushkar Hotel looking out over the holy lake with its fringe of blue-white buildings nestling beside the ghats. Pushkar had an improbable Mediterranean feel to it, a wonderfully peaceful ambience, so unlike any other place in India I had visited.

We had arrived at Ajmer in the early morning, taken the bus over Snake Mountain, and by ten o'clock were settled in a delightful double room with – luxury of luxuries – our own hot shower. Even though we were tired and grubby from the overnight journey, such was our joint obsession with each other, that no sooner had we undressed to take a shower than we found ourselves tumbling on to the bed, embroiled in a sexual frenzy.

Liana's willingness and desire to make love – wherever and whenever – was a source of constant delight to me. She was every man's fantasy, and she was mine. The only thing I found perplexing was how this stunningly sexy woman had managed to avoid the clutches of the millions of rampant males who would, like myself, have given anything to be with her. Aligned with this thought (and still suffering from the sort of self-deprecation that had become a trademark with me) was the question that, if she had been saving herself, saving that precious gift, why had she given it to me of all people? I mean, I was a nice enough guy, certainly, but Liana was *special*; she was unique. I surely was not a worthy recipient of her affections, her love, the intimacy with her body.

I kept these thoughts, bothersome though they were, pretty much to myself. I knew what Liana would say: that it was she who did not deserve such riches. I was handsome, beautiful, sexy; I was warm, loving, caring. I was a great lover. She was so lucky, she would say whenever the mood took her, so lucky to have met me.

I was bewitched, of course. It was not long before I began to believe all her words. How I kept my ego in check I'll never know. But such is the nature of enchantment. If not for this then perhaps my suspicions would have been aroused. Perhaps I would have been more concerned about the dreadful incident on our first night together. Perhaps I would have wondered about her inventiveness in the bedroom, her seemingly natural abilities, the ease with which she adapted to new positions and variations. Perhaps I would have questioned how she knew what would turn me on, and queried her skilful use of hand, tongue, lips.

But I did not. I did not give a damn.

And that in retrospect was my greatest error.

See Michael Montrose, a fool in love, with his starry eyes and stupid grin. Snigger at his ignorance, his inability to see the strings attached to each limb and the top of his head. Marvel at the skill of the marionette-master as Michael dances to a tune, not of his own making, but composed by agents beyond his understanding.

Poor Pinocchio; his head is made of wood, and he's playing with fire.

The lawn that led down to the lake was the first stretch of green grass I had seen in a month. We took off our sandals and felt the fresh, cool springiness of the blades between our toes. We ordered a pot of tea, played a game of cards and smoked cigarettes.

I had toyed with the idea of smoking whilst at university. I had bought the occasional packet of Rothmans, which would usually last a fortnight, during which time I would struggle to get the hang of breathing in the noxious fumes without coughing up bits of lung. I was not particularly successful, and after two weeks would give up and throw away the remaining fags, certain that smoking was not for me. I must have repeated this sequence of actions four or five times. I have no idea why I was so keen to smoke; it *did* seem a pretty pointless activity.

It had come as something of a surprise when on our second evening together, Liana produced a packet of cigarettes over dinner and lit up.

'I didn't know you smoked?' I said, no disapproval in my tone, just surprise.

'Just occasionally,' said Liana. 'I like to watch the

smoke curling up into the air. There's something so transient about it, the uncertainty of the spirals. It makes me think about the passing of time.'

This seemed the least likely excuse for smoking I had ever heard, but from Liana's lips it had the ring of authenticity. I did not discover until much later that Liana was a confirmed twenty-a-day addict, and that at the time she met me she had been trying to give up. By the time we arrived in Pushkar, I too was smoking like a fool. It didn't seem to matter; it was just a part of the whole, a fancy, a game. It was as irrelevant as tapping one's fingers on a table top.

The drinking, however, was another matter altogether.

17

I come from a family of teetotallers. Neither my parents nor my older sisters drink; not so much as a glass of wine with a meal. This is not, as one might suspect, for any moral or ethical reasons. They do not disapprove of alcohol; they simply don't like the taste. Consequently I was brought up in a booze-free home, and it was not until I was sixteen that I discovered the potent effect of fermented vegetable matter.

At sixteen I became a hardened cider drinker. I have, it seems, a low threshold to intoxicating substances, and I discovered in these formative years that a pint of Strongbow was enough to reduce me to a gibbering idiot. Alcohol made me popular: I was the best value entertainment in town. If you wanted an amusing evening, all you had to do was take me to the pub, pour cider down my throat, and after half an hour I would sing, dance and tell ludicrous stories for the rest of the night. Friends would happily stand me the price of a pint. While this may sound a bit demeaning, at the time I revelled in it. If girls did not fancy me for my looks, they at least liked me for my sense of humour.

I remained faithful to the sweet, sickly, gassy liquid until I attended Sussex where, as cider was considered something of a pooftah's drink, I switched to real ale. In an effort to prove I was a real man, I would drink pint after pint of the disgusting stuff in the vain hope that I would, one day, get to like it. I succeeded only in making myself very sick.

It was sweet, innocent little Jo who introduced me to the pleasures of Scotch and American Dry. It was love at first sight. At last, here was a drink that was sophisticated, pleasing in taste, easy to drink, and could get you really pissed if you so desired. Not that I liked getting drunk too often. But there were occasions when I took to the bottle with a sort of madness, determined to wipe myself out. I loved that light, carefree feeling that came at around about the fourth drink, when the tongue was loose but still in control, when everything seemed easy and amusing, and you were under the impression that everyone loved you.

My mistake, like so many drinkers, was in believing that to sustain these feelings one merely had to continue drinking, and I don't suppose, for all the throwing up I did or for all those dreadful hangovers, that I ever appreciated the fallacy of that particular theory. There comes a point, as anyone who has ever tried this knows, when reason no longer enters the picture. You are no longer in control, you no longer care. You are drunk and a potential danger to yourself and anyone who dares to come too close. The morning that I woke up to find myself in a crouched position in a strange bathroom, my knees locked, my head lodged in the toilet bowl, I realised I had a problem. Not a drink problem; drink was just the catalyst, the medium – drink was just an excuse. No, my problem was much more serious, and was to do with excess. I seemed to need *more* of everything than everyone else. More experience, more love, more care, more laughter, more pain. I wanted excess. I wanted not just to do everything, but to overdo everything. I wanted bright colours, strong flavours, pungent smells, loud music. I wanted my heart to beat faster. I wanted more respect than everyone else, more pleasure, more beauty. I never questioned whether or not I deserved it; I just knew that I had to have it, that it was necessary for my survival, essential for my well-being. Perhaps that is why, when the most beautiful woman in the world walked into my life and introduced me to the sensation of euphoria, I did not ask too many questions about whether I was deserving or not. It was what I wanted, what I needed, and that was all that really mattered.

18

From the depths of her backpack, Liana produced a full bottle of Courvoisier.

'Where have you been hiding that?'

She smiled mischievously. 'I've been saving it for a special occasion.'

'And is this a special occasion?'

'*I* think so. Don't you?'

'My life is a special occasion, since I met you,' I said. It sounded terribly pretentious, but I felt it with all sincerity.

The only drinking vessels in the room were a pair of rather unlovely glass tumblers. I washed them out as best I could, dried them on Liana's towel (which I felt was probably cleaner than my own) and returned to the bedroom, where Liana had already lit the candles, taken off her clothes, and wrapped herself in a bright, translucent *lunghi*. She uncorked the cognac, put her nose to the neck of the bottle, and drew deeply on the volatile aromas. Her eyes closed momentarily. She smiled.

I held out the glasses and she poured two large

measures. I handed her the less unpleasant of the two tumblers and we raised them to just below eye-level.

'What shall we drink to?' asked Liana. The candle flames flickered in the cross breezes, throwing dramatic shadows across the walls and ceiling.

'To us?' I suggested. 'To a world that awaits us?'

'Yes,' she said. 'That's lovely; I like that.'

We clinked glasses. I watched Liana sip from her glass, savouring the fine brandy. As I lifted the glass to my lips, Liana suddenly threw back her head and emptied the glass in one.

'Fantastic,' she said, then, seeing me standing there nonplussed, started to laugh. 'I'm sorry,' she said, 'but I love this stuff. And I don't believe in treating it with any reverence. Cognac is nothing more than good hootch in my books; the best. Come on Michael, don't just stand there gawping; we have a bottle to finish.'

By the third glass I was already feeling light-headed. Liana, however, whilst in a perfectly good mood, seemed not the least affected. I had never seen anyone drink like that. She evidently enjoyed it, but it might just as well have been grape juice for all the effect it had on her. At least, that's how it seemed at the time.

By ten o'clock the bottle was three-quarters empty. Liana was now very giggly, as indeed was I. We fooled around a little – just sexual play – but did not make love. We recounted stories of drunken debauchery; Liana said she loved getting drunk on wine and brandy, but that anything else made her sick. I told her that everything made me sick, and she thought this hysterical and laughed continuously for ten minutes until the tears streamed down her cheeks.

A small, barely perceptible change came over Liana after that. It wasn't just that she seemed to lose interest in the sex games – this didn't bother me at all, since by that time I was incapable of anything more than some rather inept fumbling – she also appeared nervous. By the time the bottle lay empty on the floor, she was looking quite distressed.

'What's wrong?' I whispered. 'What's the matter? Liana?' She looked at me as if I were a complete stranger, someone who shouldn't even be in the same room as her.

'Don't hurt me, Michael . . .'

Her face took on that terrible expression again. For a moment I thought my heart had stopped beating; surely this wasn't happening again! I had made no sharp movements, there had been nothing threatening in my tone or in the content of our conversation. There was no way she could interpret my actions as violent. This time I decided to nip this absurd idea in the bud.

'I'd never hurt you Liana. Not ever. Do you understand?' I was pretty smashed, but the urgency, the terror in her eyes had a strong sobering effect. I didn't move, I didn't reach out. Nevertheless, she shrank away from me. She looked like a small, frightened child.

'You're drunk,' she said, accusingly. 'I know what you're like when you're drunk.'

This confused me still further. 'What do you mean? You've never seen me drunk. This is the first time . . .'

'Don't get angry,' she interrupted. Her voice had that

desperate, pleading tone to it. 'Please, I'll do anything. Just don't get angry.'

'Liana, I promise you.' I wasn't sure what else to say, what else to do. I thought about getting up and leaving the room so that she wouldn't feel threatened by my presence, but I didn't like to leave her alone. I figured that if I just stayed completely still and talked to her gently, she'd see that there was nothing to worry about. It took a supreme effort of will not to reach across and put my arms around her; she looked so scared, so pathetic, all I wanted to do was hold her.

It is always on occasions such as this that the cosmos decides to show its true nature, to tease us, to make a mockery of our efforts, of our lives. After just a few minutes, with all that cognac swirling around inside me, I had a desperate need to take a leak. I knew that if I didn't do something about it swiftly, I'd probably wet myself.

'Liana, I need to use the toilet. I'm going to stand up, go to the bathroom, and then come straight back. Okay? Liana, is that okay?'

She looked at me suspiciously for a moment, then nodded.

I moved as slowly as I could, pushed myself on to my feet and tottered to the bathroom. The relief I felt was lost however beneath the hurt I felt at the indignity of the situation. My world was falling apart and all I could do was piss into a toilet bowl.

When I returned to the bedroom Liana was as I had left her. I stood in the bathroom doorway for a few moments, trying to collect my thoughts.

'Liana, I won't hurt you,' I said again. 'I couldn't hurt you. Why don't you come and sit beside me? I promise everything will be okay.'

Another rash promise. My life, sometimes, appears a frail stuttering thing, with the main protagonist lurching from one feeble oath to the next, like a spastic frog desperate to land on something real but finding only fragile lilies that will not hold his weight.

I held out my hands towards her and tried smiling. Liana just stared at me and made no efforts to reach out to me.

'What's this all about Liana? Why do you think I'm going to hurt you? I won't hurt you. I love you.'

As the words left my lips, Liana's face contorted into a snarl. 'It's always the same thing,' she spat. 'Love. I know all about your sort of love; you can't fool me with your clever words. They mean *nothing*.'

There was such hatred in her voice; it was as if I had just been run through with a sword. I felt a sharp pain slice through my chest, and then a dull ache invaded me, as if part of my soul had just died.

Until then I had thought myself, whilst not in control of the situation, at least in charge of my own emotions. But such was the hostility in Liana's voice that all of a sudden I was overwhelmed with a feeling of desperation. She did not believe me, did not trust me. I could not touch her, hold her or even speak to her. The tears welled up in my eyes and although I tried to control myself, the effort was too great. My legs felt weak, I started to shake. How much of this was due to the drink I could not have said.

All I knew was that a moment later I had sunk to my knees, head in hands, and was sobbing uncontrollably.

Sometime later – I don't know how long – I felt a hand on my shoulder. I looked up. Liana was kneeling before me. A certain calm had returned to her expression, but she looked terribly sad.

'Don't cry, Michael,' she said softly. 'Please don't cry.'

I shook my head. She put her hand to my cheek. 'Please don't cry,' she said again.

I was still so choked I could barely get the words out. 'Who did this to you Liana? Who did this terrible thing to you?'

Her eyes filled with tears. She put her arms around me, pulled me towards her, and cradled my head against her breasts.

'Poor Michael,' she said, rocking me back and forth. 'Poor, poor Michael.'

19

I have known Rachel for over twenty years. We were childhood friends. We went through school together. When I went to Sussex, Rachel continued her education at Bristol. We maintained contact during this period, although we saw each other rarely. For the last eight years, Rachel has lived in London; she is my one real link with the city. Rachel understands me better than my own family, and I am probably her closest friend.

She is a lovely woman: tall, strikingly attractive, exceptionally intelligent, very warm. She draws people of like mind and disposition around her; she has the most loyal friends of anyone I know; she is generous to a fault, and people will do anything for her. Yet she is not married and rarely has a man in tow. She has one problem, a problem that hangs over her head like the Sword of Damocles. Rachel would love to have a partner – but she hates sex. Penetration causes her extreme pain, and after intercourse she is often physically sick. Three gynaecologists have assured her that there is nothing wrong with her physically, that the sharp, shooting pains she feels are almost certainly psychosomatic, and that perhaps she should seek a different sort of professional help. Which is a great irony, since Rachel is, by profession, a psychoanalyst.

We have talked about her difficulties often, but have rarely made any headway. She says she has normal feelings of desire; she finds certain men attractive, and will often want to go to bed with them. But once she's alone with them, once clothes are removed and the first moves are made, she is overcome with a sense of panic. No matter how much she tries to control this, it is to no avail. Nine times out of ten, sex will be abandoned before it has even started, with much distress on both sides and, inevitably, dreadful recriminations.

You would think – bearing in mind her experience, connections and common sense – that Rachel might have attempted to seek advice from her professional colleagues, but she has not. When I suggested hypnosis, perhaps, as a way of discovering the source of this debilitating condition, Rachel dismissed it without rational explanation. Which is a pity, because I am certain that the key to releasing her from this prison lies buried in her past. My only evidence is something she once said to me, early one morning, whilst still half asleep.

Rachel likes sleeping with me. We can lie together in the same bed, completely naked, and there is no possibility that anything of a sexual nature will occur. We have known each other too long for that and, thankfully, are not physically attracted to each other. Even these days, if I am not abroad and Liana is not around, Rachel and I will seek each other out. It is a fine, mutual arrangement that gives us both comfort and warmth. Rachel feels safe with me; we often fall asleep in each other's arms.

After one such night I woke a little earlier than Rachel, and stayed in bed staring at the ceiling, allowing random thoughts to jostle around in my head, watching them settle to their own levels. After some five minutes of this, Rachel stirred, gave a little sniff, then snuggled up to me. She murmured a barely coherent, "Good morning," and kissed me on the chest.

'How are you feeling?' I asked, stroking her hair.

'Mmm, fine,' she mumbled. 'Strange dream.'

'What happened?'

'Not sure.'

'Tell me.'

She was still pretty dozy, so it was difficult to follow the stream-of-consciousness retelling of her dream, but the gist of it was as follows.

She was asleep in her bed, not in this flat, but in the house she had lived in as a child. She knew it was her old bedroom because of the blue and white wallpaper and the moth-eaten teddy bear that lay beside her on the pillow. Her parents had been entertaining friends and family to dinner. She had had to go to bed at eight o'clock but was not tired, and could hear them all laughing and talking in the dining room. At some point – she wasn't sure when – she heard her bedroom door open, and then heard footsteps. She saw the silhouette of her favourite uncle – her father's older brother – come towards her. He knelt down next to her and kissed her on the forehead. His breath smelt terrible; a smoky, beery smell. He whispered something in her ear but she didn't understand, and then she felt his hand under the covers. He tried to kiss her again, only this time on the lips, which she didn't like, and just as she turned her head away she felt a sharp pain in her abdomen. The pain had woken her.

It does not, I think, take either a dream specialist or an analyst to draw the obvious conclusion.

After telling me about the dream, Rachel dozed off again for an hour. When later that morning I asked her about the dream, she looked at me blankly and claimed she could remember nothing. I did not repeat what she had told me, something I still regret to this day.

20

My first thought was that someone had broken my neck. I opened my eyes to a world that I did not, initially, recognise, although it was not long before I realised that this was a problem of perspective rather than perception. I was jammed up against one end of the bed, my body twisted and contorted in a manner that I could not have devised deliberately. I could not move my head as it was crammed into the corner of the room at an angle which, I was sure, defied all natural laws. Of more immediate concern was the fact that I could not feel my left arm; it was completely numb from fingertips to elbow and, for the best part of half a minute, I succumbed to a terrible panic; I had severed a nerve, I had cut off the blood supply to my hand, I would never have the use of my arm again. What the fuck had happened to me? There was, in addition, a distinct lack of sensation in my legs, and a heavy pain in my lower back, as if I had been kicked repeatedly by an angry mule wearing jackboots. The relentless throbbing in my temples, a persistent dull thud of monotonous regularity, was offset by an unpleasant, nauseating, high-pitched whine in my left ear, which suggested that, whatever it was I had done to myself, the damage was almost certainly irreparable. As if all this were not bad enough, every time I drew breath my body was wracked by sharp pains in my chest and a hot, acidic rasping in the throat. My mouth was so dry that my tongue had become virtually immobile. Hangovers were not new to me, but this one had a personality all of its own. As all these terrible afflictions clocked on, one by one, I became more and more despondent; this was no way to start the day, any day.

Liana was fast asleep beside me, snoring heavily. She looked peaceful enough, and had managed to remain unknotted for her night's journey into dreams; I was just the slightest bit envious, and noted, even in my reduced state, a desire to wake her roughly and blame her for my ills. But I did not wake her. Instead, drawing on whatever internal resources were still left to me, I got out of bed – carefully – and staggered to the bathroom. A journey of a thousand miles starts with one step, according to some know-it-all Chinaman. What he didn't say is that sometimes a journey of just five yards can start with tripping up over your own foot, and finish a few moments later, the intended destination still a lifetime away. I had neglected to take into account just how numb my legs were, and their refusal to pay attention to instructions from the central nervous system was a crushing blow to me so early in the morning. I did not dare risk another fall; I was feeling so fragile by this stage that I figured one more dive and I would shatter into a million pieces. I crawled the rest of the way to the bathroom, co-ordinating hand and knee with great effort. Had I been able to appreciate it more, I'd have realised what a fascinating experiment this was in regression; I was being given the opportunity to experience, with the consciousness of an adult, just what it felt like as a baby to become independently mobile for the first time. Unfortunately, such appreciation was sadly absent that morning so by way of compensation I had to settle for the sense of achievement that accompanied my having reached the bathroom without further mishap.

Although we had hot water, I opted for a cold shower in the hope of reviving my aching head and suffering body. The Chinese (there they are again) believe that a shower not only cleanses the body but invigorates the spirit. As a general rule this may hold, most of the time, but it is not, alas, a universal law, as anyone observing me that morning would have seen for themselves. I left the bathroom feeling even more battered than when I had entered. Whereas before I had been merely in agony and wanting to die, now I was cold, wet, in agony, and wanted to die an especially quick death. It took further extraordinary efforts to dress myself, as every limb felt like it was encased in a plaster cast. My vision was none too clear either, so I have no idea whether or not I left the room in a decent state.

The sun was neither warm nor beautiful that morning, just mean and angry. I made my way, delicately, to the hotel lawn, sat down on a comfortable cane chair beside a small marble table and ordered some breakfast. I was immediately thankful that Pushkar was a holy City and therefore strictly vegetarian, so I could not order fried eggs which in India are certain to be served burnt on the bottom, uncooked on the top, swimming in a glutinous amalgam of fat and albumen, and guaranteed to make you feel sick, even if you were in perfect health when you started the day. I settled instead for tea and toast.

The toast was unusual; I think the cooks in the kitchen had waved the slice of bread somewhere in the vicinity of the flames for a moment, and then soaked the lukewarm bread in something resembling animal fat. The tea was good, if you like that sort of thing. They have a unique way of making tea in India; one would be hard pressed to devise a method better suited to totally ruining one of the finest drinks in the world. Take a large kettle, fill it with cold water, tea leaves, milk and sugar, put it on the flames and wait for the whole lot to boil, then strain through an oily rag, and *voilà*, *chai*! It's an acquired taste; one with which, thankfully, I had already become very familiar.

I drank tea, relaxed as best I could, and slowly but surely the aches and pains subsided. I regained full feeling in my arms and legs, my back felt less sore, and the percussion section of the Hangover Ensemble downed instruments. It had always amazed me just how resilient the human body was, how well it recovered after a damn good thrashing. It also occurred to me that morning that, at the grand age of twenty-one, I was getting too old for this sort of shit.

By the time an hour had passed, I had begun to feel

more like a living, human being. I ordered some more tea, and a few moments later Liana joined me.

'Hi,' she said, a little sheepishly, leant over and kissed me on the nose.

'Good morning. How are you feeling?'

She lowered herself gently on to the chair. 'Hmmm... not too bad. A little hungover, but nothing serious. You?'

I wanted to launch into a full description of just how I had been feeling, but even thinking about it made me feel slightly queasy. 'Better than an hour ago. My head hurts; I'm not used to cognac.'

'Did we finish the bottle?'

'Uh-huh.'

'Oops. Well, never mind. It was fun, anyway.'

I did not say anything then as it simply did not seem appropriate. But after Liana had ordered herself some tea and toast, I broached the subject of her behaviour.

'Liana, it wasn't really fun at all, was it.'

'Wasn't it? Oh... did I do something awful?'

'Don't you remember?'

Liana shrugged. 'I remember laughing a lot when you told me everything made you sick. The rest is a bit of a blur. Oh dear, what did I say? Was I horrible?'

'No... well, you became terribly upset. Don't you remember?'

She shook her head. 'Probably the drink. Take no notice, I often get a bit stupid when I'm drunk. Whatever I said or did, it's nothing to worry about.' She reached across and took my hand: 'Really, Michael.'

I sighed, rather too loudly I suspect, and held her hand

more firmly. This really didn't ring true at all. She had not been drunk on that first night, and her reaction had not been all that different under the influence of the cognac. I did not know what to think.

We held hands and stared out across the lake until Liana's breakfast arrived. She devoured the lot in about five minutes, exclaiming how famished she was. Her mood was light, normal, and in the early morning sun Liana looked as beautiful, as ravishing, as the day I met her. She bore no resemblance to the frightened creature who had scuttled into the corner of the room the previous night, and if anyone had seen us sitting there they would never have guessed that we were anything other than a young, happy, loving couple.

When Liana had finished eating, she let out a small, satisfied sigh.

'Well,' she said. 'What shall we do first? Go for a walk or make love?' She slipped her hand out of mine and laid it gently on my thigh. She gave me her best "come-on" look, and applied a little pressure to my groin.

There was, as my American friends would have said, no contest.

21

I have nothing against marriage. Some of my best friends are married. So, for that matter, am I.

Adam and Emma have been married for five years. I went to university with them, and we have been close friends ever since then. They did the usual travelling/loafing about/finding themselves bit after graduating. They went their separate ways for a while, but eventually came back to each other and decided to live together for a year before taking the plunge. Adam started up his own business, Emma went into management consultancy. They made a packet. They bought a beautiful home in Gloucestershire. Adam sold his business, took a less stressful day job, banked the profits. And after three years, having found emotional and financial security, they did the only thing that two intelligent, attractive, well-balanced people could do.

They had a baby.

Daniel is now two years old. I have watched him grow from being a beautiful blue-eyed, blond-haired, chubby-cheeked bundle of fat and dribble, into a beautiful blue-eyed, blond-haired tearaway. Emma took to motherhood in a way that surprised everyone who knew her. She now has no wish to go back to work, and seems disgracefully content to spend all her time with her little pride and joy. Adam often leaves work early, or takes a long weekend so that he can play with his charming son. They are wonderful with him. He has inherited his father's brains and stamina, his mother's good looks and temperament. He will receive love, attention and care in abundance. He will have the smartest clothes, the flashiest toys, the best education. Adam and Emma will take him abroad on his first holidays, and he will never be short of money. As soon as he is old enough to drive, Adam will buy him his first car (I know) and look forward with eager anticipation to the day when he brings home his first girlfriend, of whom, no doubt, Emma will disapprove, but say nothing. He will pass all his scholastic examinations with flying colours, secure a place at the university of his choice, and never have to struggle with his studies. Men will wish to be seen in his company, and women will swoon as he walks by. Then, one day, he will turn around to his parents and tell them that they are complacent, middle-class capitalists with no sense of community and a value system that is both vacuous and selfish. And Adam and Emma will – whilst suffering the torment of rejection – torture themselves with the question, "Where did we go wrong?", to which, of course, there is only one answer.

I look at young Daniel, his brilliant golden locks and sparkling sky-blue eyes, running around the living room, and a twinge of something like envy settles on me like an invisible shroud. I watch the way he climbs over the furniture on his little adventures, pursuing imaginary monsters that cannot scare him, cannot harm him, because he has magical powers, because he is safe. I watch the way Emma coos over him, revels in his company, and I think of the years of sacrifice ahead, of the oodles of love she will give to this little human being.

And I see the look in the boy's eyes when Adam walks in the room; the excitement, the adoration, the complete, unquestioning trust as Daniel runs towards his kneeling father and throws his arms around his neck. And when I hear him say, "Kiss me, Daddy," a lump comes to my throat, and all I want to do is cry.

22

The following week passed without incident. Pushkar was such a sleepy, pleasant town that we did not feel inclined to move on, and had it not been for the imminent arrival of hordes of people we might have stayed for weeks. As it was, during the following few days Pushkar began to gear up for the forthcoming *mela*, an immense festival known familiarly as the Cattle Fair. We talked to a few of the locals about the fair, and they all said the same thing; we should stay, it was an amazing sight, there would be thousands coming. The idea of a cattle fair did not sound particularly inspiring, and I could not at first understand why it was such a huge attraction. The gathering of the Rajasthani clans was, however, more than just a chance to trade a few camels. According to Hindu belief, bathing in the lake during *Kartik Purnima*, the full moon, absolves one from a lifetime's accumulated sins. Hindus would be making their way to Pushkar from all over Northern India, and the population would swell from three thousand to over two hundred thousand.

Sure enough, the town soon became more crowded,

room prices started to soar and, although the fair was supposed to be one of the most colourful events of the season, neither of us felt we could cope with the crowds. We decided that we would move on the eve of the fair. In the meantime we took advantage of Pushkar's many pleasures; we ate and slept, went for long walks, watched the sunset, played card games, told stories, made love.

We had fallen, if not into a routine, then certainly into a pattern. There seemed to be no question that we were going to carry on travelling together, that we were partners, that we would stay together. These things were all naturally assumed. Liana was my new girlfriend. We were in love. Simple as that.

These were easy, relaxed days, with no pressures, no external restrictions. We did not feel obliged to sightsee, or do anything specific for that matter. We would sit for hours at restaurants and just talk about this and that. We probably learnt more about each other's backgrounds during that week than in any period that followed. As I had already gathered, Liana had had a pretty conventional middle-class upbringing. The eldest of two children – she had a brother two years her junior – she had been educated at an undistinguished comprehensive school in Surrey (her parents, whilst well off, were committed quasi-socialists). She had taken 'A' levels in Art, English and History, before going on to study Fine Art at Kent University. She was not, she said, either academically bright or especially talented – she often referred to herself as run-of-the-mill – but felt she made the most of what little she had.

Her closest friend was a girl called Anne; they had attended the same school together, pretty much grown up in each other's homes. Anne had not gone on to further education, but taken a secretarial course and was now working as a P.A. to the managing director of a small publishing company based in Surrey. They were still very close and saw each other as often as time and circumstances allowed. Liana believed Anne to be the kindest and most honest person she had ever known. There wasn't an evil bone in her body, said Liana; she was "very together". She knew what she wanted, knew how to get it. She was wonderful.

Other friends were mentioned, but it was obvious that none held the same special place in Liana's affections. Oddly, she didn't mention any friends from her university days. When I questioned her about this she just shrugged her shoulders dismissively and muttered something about the students not being her sort of people. She didn't want to elaborate, so I didn't push her.

Liana was very fond of her mother and father. They sounded like model parents. They had been loving without smothering her, encouraging without being pushy, and generous without ever spoiling her. She had a great deal of respect for them. Where other people's parents would have balked at the idea of their only daughter going to India, her folks had been very supportive. They were, naturally, a bit concerned, and they had asked a lot of questions; her father had even done some "independent research", just so that he knew what Liana could expect. They had even given her some spending money so that she could have a little comfort now and then. They sounded like lovely people.

An objective listener might well have been a little suspicious of this all-too-perfect background – the supportive, loving parents, the delightful best friend, the easy untroubled schooldays – it was all so normal.

Not like real life at all.

On the eve of the fair we decided to see what was happening in the valley beyond the town, as this was supposed to be its main site. We walked around the far side of the lake, away from the town, through some nondescript fields, past a few of Pushkar's several hundred temples, and up a shallow rise that hid from view the valley that lay beyond. Such was the peace and simplicity of this area that we were quite unprepared for the sight that greeted us as we hit the top of the rise.

'My God,' said Liana. 'It's like something out of the Bible.'

'The book or the film?'

Liana poked her tongue out at me. 'Film, silly; who reads books these days?'

The nomads and their camels had arrived. Not hundreds, not thousands, but tens of thousands; in fact, as far as the eye could see, camels of every size and colour from off-white through grey, brown, khaki and black, stretched to the horizon. This was truly a sea of camels. And in between the *mélange* of desert hues one could pick out the brilliant flashes of red, yellow and orange, the luminous turbans of the rakish Rajasthanis. In the distance, an endless line of tents had been set up, a new village especially for the visitors. And beyond, being put through their paces for the days that followed, camels raced across the flat, sandy plains. An awesome spectacle.

That night I dreamt of snake charmers, dancing wenches, and fires in the desert.

23

I have always been puzzled by pain. There are too many things that I do not understand about it. We are told that physical pain is the body's way of telling us that something is wrong. Pain is a defence mechanism. Okay, I'll buy that. I know what a toothache's like, that if I don't get my teeth fixed the damage could get worse. That's fine. What is less clear to me is: what, exactly, is it that's hurting? I say "My tooth hurts", but that's nonsense. It isn't the tooth that is hurting, it's me. *I* am in pain. Not my body; me. It seems to me that pain is not so much a defence mechanism as Nature's way of telling us that, however rational we'd like to think we are, no matter how much we try to dismiss the idea, we all have a soul, something that is not corporeal, the essence of self, something that hurts when there is pain. This is why painkillers and anaesthetics are such amazing things. Somehow they manage to insert a barrier between body and soul so that, whilst the body may be still damaged, the soul does not have to suffer.

You're not convinced by this argument. Okay. Let's go

back to the first idea. Pain is a necessary function to ensure we don't fuck our bodies up completely, to stop us walking on sprained ankles or accidentally setting fire to ourselves. Like I said, I'm prepared to accept that. But what about the other sort of pain; the pain of heartbreak, the pain of loss, of disappointment? We've all suffered that pain. It hurts like hell, and there are no really effective painkillers to ease the hurt (although copious amounts of alcohol may effect temporary relief). This time though, there's nothing external we can point to. We can't say "My tooth hurts, not me". We can only say "Me. Me. *I'm* hurting, *I'm* in pain".

And whenever this happens, whenever I suffer that sort of pain, I'm faced with the same question. What purpose does it serve? What use is this pain? The hurt I feel when someone I love passes away does not stop others close to me from dying. It is no defence, no early warning system. All it does is make me feel awful, miserable, tearful, depressed; it makes me cynical and hopeless. It makes me feel that life, after all, is not really worth living.

So, perhaps, that's where the answer lies. Emotional pain is Nature's way of ensuring we don't enjoy life too much, don't get too attached to it, too fond of it, so that when death comes, as it must, we don't feel cheated. If this is the case, if all that pain is just to make sure we don't turn around and start complaining when the grim reaper starts knocking on the door, then I'd prefer a different arrangement. Give me a disclaimer to sign. Right now. I promise not to get pissed off with anyone when it's my turn to die. I won't shout and scream, I won't get angry, I won't complain, I won't ask for my money back. In return, free me from this awful thing called pain. I've had enough. I've learnt my lesson. I understand: life's no great shakes, it's only short, and very soon it will all be over.

See? I really do understand.

24

Agra, home of the Taj Mahal, was a great disappointment to us after the ease and pleasures of Pushkar. It was a noisy, aggressive city full of rip-off merchants and unfriendly natives. Agra had been a tourist destination for too long, and the locals saw every visitor as a candidate for fleecing. We stayed only long enough to view the main attraction, then departed swiftly on the overnight train to Benares. But not before the damage had been done. Liana was touched-up no less than three times during our twenty-four-hour stay in this miserable excuse for a city, and on the third occasion she lost her temper so completely, with such vehemence, that I felt sure she was going to attack physically the greasy, pathetic little man who had violated her. I don't believe I've ever seen anyone so angry and upset, and for several hours after the incident, Liana was still visibly shaken.

I tried my best to calm her down, commiserating with her over the offence whilst at the same time trying to keep the whole thing in perspective, but Liana was having none of it; she was furious, and wanted to remain that way. If anyone had dared touch her during the remainder of the day, they'd have been dead meat.

The second-class sleeper was packed for the journey eastwards, and neither of us slept well. Consequently we arrived in Benares the following evening, jaded and tetchy, only to find the autorickshaw drivers giving us as hard a time as their colleagues in Agra had done. We were too tired to fight it, so allowed one particularly disreputable-looking driver to take us to the hotel of his choice. Thankfully, the place was clean and relatively inexpensive, and rarely had a bed looked so inviting. We collapsed into a semi-comatose state at about nine that night and slept right through until ten the next morning.

Although she woke refreshed from her long night's sleep, Liana was still in a foul mood the following morning. Whether the Agra experience was actually responsible for her change of heart, or merely a catalyst, I could not tell. All I knew was that, suddenly, Liana was sick of India. She'd had enough.

We walked around the town that day. I tried to stay cheerful and optimistic, but this had no effect on her. Scenes that had previously seemed fascinating to Liana were now dismissed as ugly. What had once been lively and electric was now just crowded and dirty. She was fed up with the people, sick of the food. She wanted to go home.

The change in Liana was so dramatic that it caught me completely off guard. I thought, perhaps, that fatigue had coloured her feelings, and tried to suggest that we should just take it easy for a couple of days, but even this idea was shot down in flames. As the day wore on, Liana became more and more miserable; by nightfall she had become quite tearful, and I realised there was only one solution.

We would have to go home.

I slept poorly that night, waking several times. At around five in the morning, I woke for the final time. I knew there was no way I would get back to sleep, so I got out of bed quietly – Liana was still fast asleep – washed swiftly and threw on some clothes.

Out on the street the rickshaw drivers were already gathering in the cold morning darkness, waiting to catch the fresh shoals of travellers that keep them fed. Laxman, a small, elderly Hindu with a roguish, gap-toothed smile, asked me if I wanted to go down to the river; he explained in his broken English that the sun would be rising soon, and that it was a good time to see the Ganges. I knew Liana would be in no mood for sightseeing, so having agreed a price I allowed Laxman to peddle me down to the ghats, the stepped banks of the holy river, where I negotiated for a boat and boatman. The sun had yet to appear and despite a cool breeze, wafting across from the river, I was still half asleep, and don't suppose I conducted the most impressive piece of bargaining.

We set off southwards. *Dhobi wallahs* and a few eager bathers were already on the ghats, the former belting all manner of dirt out of the laundry by swinging it against large flat stones, the latter braving the cold, filthy water. My boatman explained that this would be the first of up to five ritual bathes that day. A thick, unappealing scum floated on the surface, beneath which a still, murky green fluid appeared to ferment. The sun, red and cool, lifted above the horizon. A rotting cow carcass drifted by. I wondered what sort of dedication was required to bathe in this water five times a day.

A few other boats glided slowly along the river; an eerie quiet, attenuated sound and action. Benares was waking slowly, in much the same way, I suspected, as it had done for thousands of years. At the southernmost ghat the boat turned. By the time we reached the northern stretch, the river had sprung to life. Here were scenes of unparalleled fascination. For a few minutes I began to doubt the wisdom of my decision to return home; where else in the world would one ever come across scenes like these? And it wasn't just the hordes of men, women and children involved in their daily rituals that appealed. All along the banks of the Ganges stood a collection of innumerable styles of building, heaped up in stacks, all in various stages of decay. The overall appearance was one of unreality, as if someone had constructed a set for some hybrid oriental/medieval/science-fiction movie, with towers, balustrades, balconies, temples, turrets and windowless walls rising resplendently towards the brilliant blue sky, a sublime backdrop of colour and form, before which the extraordinary ritual of mass-bathing was played out with solemnity, abandonment, fastidiousness and great humour.

At Manikarnika ghat, the last embers of a cremation smoked spookily as a huge pile of ashes overflowed unceremoniously into the river. Four pallbearers carried a cloth-wrapped body supported on a stretcher down the steps and immersed it in the river. As the stretcher was lifted clear, a bloody torrent poured from the corpse, and my stomach turned as the reddened pool collected ominously on the still surface of the waters. Body and soul were two very distinct concepts here; the bloody, rotting corpse had been just a vehicle, a container, and now that it was empty, it meant nothing. The soul had departed, so the body could be consigned to the flames without a second thought. I had never seen a dead body up close before, and certainly never witnessed a cremation. Somehow, watching the flesh catch fire, seeing how matter-of-fact this all was to the Hindus, made me realise how pointless and wasteful are the ceremonies we have in the West for despatching our dead. This was surely the more sensible way.

I arrived back at the hotel just as Liana was waking up. I was still confused about her change of heart, but I didn't tell her about where I'd been or what I'd seen; somehow I knew it would be the wrong thing to do. Instead, I took off my clothes, slid into bed beside her, and kissed her on the nose.

'Good morning.'
'Hi. Where have you been?'
'Just for a walk. How are you feeling?'
'Lonely.'
'Lonely?'
'Mmm. I woke up and you weren't here.'
'I'm sorry love; I couldn't sleep, and I didn't want to wake you.'

Liana put her arms around me and kissed me. 'I'll always want you to be there Michael . . . when I wake up. Tell me you'll always be there.' There was a plaintive tone to her voice; for a moment I thought she might cry.

'I promise,' I said, and spent the rest of the day wondering why I found it so easy to promise the impossible.

25

Most people seem to possess certain mechanisms – either inherent or acquired – to help protect themselves from severe emotional trauma. In their relationships and interactions with other people they act with a degree of caution, they always hold back – even in close relationships – so that there is a part of themselves that is safe, untouched; something to fall back on when, after the love has gone, they are on their own again.

I was born without such a self-protection mechanism, neither did I acquire it in my youth. Perhaps it was all that love and affection showered on me as a child. Who knows? Either way, it has left me extremely vulnerable, and when I hurt, when I suffer, it seems to take on a quality quite unlike anything other people have experienced. When love turns sour and a relationship looks about to destroy itself under the internal tensions, I become a desperate man. The thought that someone might leave me fills me with dread – a sort of existential horror of being alone – and I would rather suffer any amount of torment than submit to that. Even in the final stages of the break-up, you will see me snatching and clutching at anything and everything like a drowning man clinging to the wreckage. It is a pathetic sight; a man so desperate not to be on his own that he will demean himself and tolerate words and actions so hurtful that anyone witnessing his behaviour would pronounce him mad. This madness extends into other areas of my life. One way in which it manifests itself is that perennial curse of the insecure, the obsessive neurotic's *bête noir*; jealousy.

Unlike envy, which I had experienced in one form or another for most of my adolescence, sexual jealousy had eluded me because, of course, I never had anything to be jealous of. Until I met Jo. Going out with an attractive woman can be fraught with danger for someone who has yet to understand the nature of his own obsessive tendencies. On the one hand, I found Jo attractive and sexy, and enjoyed finding her so. On the other hand, Jo's attraction was not limited solely to myself. Initially I derived a certain proprietorial pleasure from watching other men eye her up and down, wishing they were sleeping with her, but such pleasure was short-lived, and I have my good friend Richard to thank for that.

I had been going out with Jo for about six months when the troubles began. We were lying in bed one night, side by side, holding hands in the aftermath of our lovemaking. It was always a supremely peaceful time; after sex, I always felt clear, becalmed, and would allow my mind to drift wherever it wanted. On this occasion, and for no particular reason, I recalled a story Richard had told me that day concerning one of the Social Science tutors, a scurrilous piece of gossip that I'd found both amusing and intriguing. I began to tell Jo the story, but no sooner had I mentioned Richard's name than she began to get irritated.

'What's up, Jo? What's the matter?' I asked, squeezing her hand slightly.

'Nothing,' said Jo, the word snapping like a broken rubber band.

'Come on. Tell me.'

Jo sighed. 'I'm sick to death of hearing about Richard, that's all. Honestly Michael, he's all you ever talk about. It's Richard this and Richard that . . . I just don't think it's very healthy to be so preoccupied with him.'

'Healthy?'

'He's a bad influence.'

'What?'

'You heard.' Jo leant over to the bedside table and turned on the light. I sat up in bed, puzzled and a little shocked by the outburst. Jo never had a bad word for anyone, and she'd certainly never mentioned Richard before in anything other than the most benign of terms.

'What is this, Jo? You've never said anything to me before about it. I had no idea you felt so strongly.'

Jo shrugged. She was evidently feeling very uncomfortable having brought the subject up. 'I didn't want to say anything. I know he's your closest friend, and I didn't want to upset you. In fact, I wish I hadn't said anything now.'

'You should have said something earlier.' I took her hand again and squeezed it gently, but Jo did not respond. There was a moment's uncomfortable silence, during which time it dawned on me that Jo's comments were no mere spontaneous outburst. There was almost certainly more to this than met the eye. I could tell from her expression that something had been left unsaid.

'Tell me,' I said at last.

'Tell you what?' Jo's ingenuousness was often appealing, but when she was faking it was just aggravating.

'What happened, Jo. What did Richard do?'

'I didn't say he'd done anything.'

'Come on Jo, don't do this to me. Just tell me what he did.'

Jo's eyes started to fill with tears. 'It wasn't what he did, it's what he tried to do. He's a right bastard, Michael. He's not to be trusted.'

I must have suspected right then what had happened, but for those few faltering moments before Jo related the story I tried to banish from my mind such thoughts. It all seems terribly trivial now, but by the time Jo had finished telling me about what had happened, I was beside myself with fury.

Basically, Richard had taken advantage of my absence one weekend (I had gone home to visit my folks) to pay a friendly call on Jo, to make sure she wasn't lonely or anything like that. Jo had no reason to suspect that this was anything other than a casual visit – her boyfriend's best mate coming over out of the goodness of his heart et cetera. He had even brought a bottle of wine. She hadn't realised that he was fairly well oiled on arrival, so by the time they'd polished off the Soave, Richard was pretty pissed. And it was then that he tried to persuade Jo to go to bed with him. Jo thought he was just joking around, so for a while she played along with it. Richard had interpreted this reaction as serious intent, and so when Jo explained that she was very flattered but no thanks, Richard thought this was just a come-on, and made a lunge for her. That's when Jo realised it wasn't just a game and asked Richard to leave. He refused at first and then started to get aggressive, at which point Jo threatened to scream the place down. He left.

That I was shocked by this tale will be of no surprise. What was unexpected was the extent of my anger. It was one thing for a complete stranger to start chatting up your girlfriend at a party, but when your closest friend plans a deliberate, premeditated assault . . .

Of course, it was Jo who became the focus of my anger. Such was my reluctance to believe that Richard would do such a thing that I even accused Jo of having led him on. It was a foul accusation and not surprisingly it reduced her to tears. It was only then that my anger dissipated and I saw how cruel and selfish I had been. Jo had tried to protect me from knowing about the incident because she knew how much I respected and cared about Richard, how I effectively idolised him, and she had not wanted to burst my bubble. She had no wish to come between two friends, and if I hadn't mentioned Richard's name that night – and assuming there was no repetition of the incident – perhaps it would never have come to light. But it had come to light and, for me, things would never be the same.

From that moment on, every male under sixty was a potential rapist, trying to get inside *my* girlfriend's knickers (note the possessive form). If I came across Jo so much as talking to another man I became obsessed with the idea that Jo was being propositioned. I even turned on some poor unsuspecting bloke who had simply stopped Jo in the street one day to ask directions. Jo initially thought that this was just a passing phase, a reaction to the news of Richard's behaviour, so at first she said nothing. But as the months passed she become more concerned over my increasingly jealous behaviour and eventually, after a particularly violent argument, issued me with an ultimatum. Either I started behaving reasonably and rationally, or else she would leave me. It was the only time she ever issued a threat to me. I treated it with the gravity it deserved.

Externally, I managed to curb the more extravagant manifestations of the curse. I no longer interrupted conversations Jo had with other men; I did not make a show of proprietorial dancing every time a man walked by, and I stopped giving Jo the third degree at the end of every day. Instead, I kept my jealousy to myself, locked away in some dark, damp recess of the mind where it festered like a septic wound.

And it is with me still.

26

I was not due to return to England for three weeks; Liana, in theory, had another month, but with her disenchantment so advanced there seemed no question of continuing the trip. I could see no point in carrying on alone. Travel had taken second place to love; I had met the woman of my dreams, and I was not about to let her go, not for a moment. Wherever Liana wanted to go, whatever she wanted to do, that would be fine with me. There was nothing I would not do for her.

Once the decision had been taken to return home Liana's mood brightened considerably. She tried, rather half-heartedly, to persuade me to stay and finish the trip, but I was adamant that I wanted to go back with her. She did not put up much in the way of resistance.

We organised train tickets back to Delhi for the following day. I was not sure what would happen when we arrived; we both had open returns, albeit on different airlines, and I knew nothing about the procedure for changing flights, but I figured we'd sort that out in Delhi.

That evening we had a little celebration, although what we were celebrating was never made completely clear; I think it had something to do with returning to normality, although I wouldn't want to say for sure.

We were staying in the old quarter of Benares, a fascinating maze of narrow alleyways crammed with stalls and shops which never seemed to close. We decided to try and find a recommended restaurant that was, supposedly, hidden somewhere amid this bristling labyrinth, and so armed only with a scrap of paper on which someone had written indecipherable hieroglyphics that claimed to show the way, we headed out into the night. It was only after the sun had set that the old city really came to life; lights were strung up along the streets, and the entire place buzzed with a noisy excitement. Shopkeepers beckoned us to examine their wares, young women giggled as we passed by, hand in hand, and the occasional beggar held up a scrawny hand for alms. Spicy odours wafted from darkened doorways, and little children chased each other in and out of the shops. It was such a vibrant, colourful display that I could not understand why Liana should want to leave it so suddenly. However, I knew better than to question her further on this point, and instead tried to soak up as much of the atmosphere as I could.

It took us about twenty minutes to find the restaurant, a rather dingy-looking place located behind one of the thousands of temples that seemed to exist at every intersection. There were a couple of locals chatting excitedly in one corner, and two travellers who looked up and smiled at us as we entered. There was no menu as such, just a set *thali* meal, consisting of several dishes of well-cooked spicy vegetables, a stack of chapatis, the ubiquitous lentil dahl and the inevitable boiled rice. It was as traditional a meal as you could get in India, the sort of thing you could find at any roadside stall or shack, and at first I couldn't understand why this place had been especially recommended. However, once we began to eat it soon became clear that the food was indeed more flavoursome and of a higher quality than any we had tried previously. Whereas curried vegetables all tended to taste the same after a while, these dishes were delicately spiced, each with its own very distinctive aroma. The chapatis were light, freshly made and did not taste of chewy cardboard, and even the dahl was more substantial than usual. The meal was also plentiful and extremely cheap; as soon as a dish became empty it was refilled with more of the same.

We ate with great gusto, perhaps aware that it would be one of our last genuine Indian meals. I was especially pleased to see Liana in such high spirits. We talked about all manner of things over dinner, but at some point in the evening Liana suddenly became terribly apologetic about her decision to leave India. She tried to explain that she had always been very moody, prone to wild swings in temperament, which she jokingly put down to "the artist" in her. So changeable was she that friends at school had nicknamed her "Weather", a neat double pun, as no one was ever sure whether her mood would be good or bad. I told Liana that she wasn't to worry, that I understood, that none of that mattered, that India wasn't about to disappear, that I could revisit it another time. All I cared about was her happiness.

We didn't say much to each other as we wandered back slowly to our guest house. Liana seemed lost in thoughts of home, and I, whilst pleased at some level to be returning, was also a little concerned about the decision. Until that moment I had not thought about what we would do on our return to England, without jobs or money, and the only accommodation available to us our respective parents' homes. As on so many subsequent occasions, I had given little thought to the consequences of my actions and decisions, but carried on like a blind, trusting fool, treading where the angels feared, waltzing with the dragons. I had always been impulsive, prepared to try anything, do anything, to climb trees, walk out on to fragile branches, jump up and down; but with Liana beside me, I had gone one step further and become fearless.

Or perhaps just plain stupid.

If you're prepared to forgive a twenty-one-year-old for his ambition, his egocentricity, his self-assurance, then surely you can stretch your forgiveness to take in his lack of experience, his wide-eyed wonder, his naïve fearlessness. What did I know back then? I was in love.

It's not much of a defence, but then again, I hadn't actually committed any crime – other than being too hopeful, too optimistic, too trusting.

Delhi was as insane as when I had seen it for the first time just a few weeks previously. It had none of the charm of the Rajasthan cities and I was worried that if we had to spend more than a day or two here Liana might go to pieces. She seemed so terribly vulnerable; I so wanted to take care of her, keep her from harm. As it was, her mood was still very positive, and she seemed unperturbed by the very sights that had begun to aggravate her in Benares. Like a prisoner who has been told she will be out on parole in a matter of days, Liana was full of energy and excitement. She couldn't stop talking about all the things we could do together once we were back home. She would get a job in advertising or graphics, something like that, just for a short while so that we could afford to rent a place of our own. She would illustrate my travel articles and we'd sell them to all the major newspapers and magazines and make enough money to go on another trip next year. Her parents would help out financially if we were stuck. I could start work on a novel – I did want to write a novel, didn't I? – and she would spend her spare time painting and drawing; perhaps she could interest a gallery in selling her works. Everything would work out fine, she was sure; after all, we were happy and in love. What more could we ask for?

The airline offices were amazingly accommodating and managed to book Liana on to a flight for the following day. I would have to wait a further twenty-four hours, which did not seem too great a hardship. We spent the rest of our time together in a supercharged state of excitement, and by the time I saw Liana on to her flight, with tears streaming down her face, I knew that nothing could stop us from being together, from having the best of all possible lives.

As you know, I only got it half right.

27

Yesterday was another bad day for Liana. She's been counting, and realised that there are just ten days left before I have to leave, before she must return to The Sanctuary. She broke down at breakfast time and started sobbing, pleading with me not to go, not to leave her. There was nothing I could do or say; she was inconsolable. There is always the danger when she gets like this that she will do damage to herself, and I have to watch her like a hawk at these times. It does no good to hide the knives and the aspirin – she may not necessarily make a suicide attempt. Often it is something much more banal, like trying to slam her hand in the door, or burning her wrists with lighted cigarettes (a favourite of hers; she claims she doesn't feel the pain until afterwards, until long after the hairs have been singed and the flesh seared). I won't keep alcohol in the house any more, though. It's far and away the worst depressant for Liana. Last year she managed to find half a bottle of Scotch that I'd completely forgotten about – it was hidden behind some books – and she polished off the lot in less than an hour. I found her, smashed out of her head, trying to set fire to the mattress.

The doctors at The Sanctuary say there's no possible hope for Liana, that recovery is out of the question, and that containment is the best that can be hoped for. They have tried to persuade me on numerous occasions that she should become a full-time resident, but apart from the prohibitive expense, I cannot see how this will benefit her at all. Despite the horrendous problems of coping with a madwoman for six months of the year, at least when she's with me she gets to live a little. In The Sanctuary she just vegetates; watches television, reads the occasional magazine, does endless crossword puzzles. She will paint just two or three pictures in all that time. Here in London she gets to see our friends, go out to dinner, the movies, the occasional play. She goes shopping, takes in an art or photography exhibition now and then and leads – at least for a short while – the nearest she will ever come to a normal life. If that were to be taken away from her she'd have nothing. She'd just decay. To see her after six months in that place is a heartbreaking sight. She is calm, certainly; almost docile. Like someone who has completely given up on life, she has the appearance of a ghost – frail, almost translucent. Her hair is lank, her eyes are dull, her lips cracked and dry. After a week with me in London, she becomes transformed. We buy new clothes; we go to the hairdresser, the manicurist, the solarium. We buy make-up, shoes, perfumes. Like a withering plant that is finally given water and sustenance, Liana bursts once again into life, becoming her old, radiant self. That is when we start to visit friends. Liana sparkles like a polished diamond on these occasions, her fast wit eager to engage with the people she most cares about. And of course, she looks as ravishing as ever; in fact, in my eyes, as Liana heads towards mid-life, she has taken on an even more alluring beauty, a mature sophistication that, whilst no longer setting the heart off at a gallop, lingers insidiously in the mind. It is a beauty that is recalled long after she has disappeared from view.

Keeping up the pretence is particularly hard work, especially with our oldest friends like Adam and Emma. After all, where exactly does Liana go for the winter? We have a simple but clever lie. Devon: an artists' colony, a retreat, way out in the heart of the countryside, where she paints and sculpts and enjoys the company of like-minded people. And as if to add credence to the lie, whenever we go visiting Liana always brings along one of her paintings. She is still immensely gifted in this field, and her work, which is easily accessible, always elicits words of praise and admiration from our friends which, of course, Liana adores. To see her, if only for one evening, basking in the warmth and love of these true companions, to see her happy, laughing, is worth all the sorrow and hardship that invariably follows. For a few hours once, maybe twice a week, Liana can be completely normal and content, without fear or terror, and there is no price one can put on such a thing.

28

My parents greeted my return home with a mixture of shock, surprise and delight. I had not had time whilst in Delhi to call them – everything had been so rushed – and besides, trying to place an international call from India was something of a hit and miss affair at the best of times.

When my parents asked me why I had returned early, I stalled them, saying only that my trip had been great, that I'd had a wonderful time, but that it was all a bit overwhelming. I cited exhaustion as the main reason for leaving India, and if you had seen the state of me when I arrived back you would not have doubted it for a moment.

I was tired, jetlagged and dirty, but as soon as I'd managed to convince Mum and Dad that I was alive and well, I made my excuses and went out to phone Liana. I could have made the call from home, but that would have entailed explanations, and I did not consider it the right time for love stories.

I could barely contain my excitement as I raced up the High Road to the phone box. It had only been a day or two since I'd last seen Liana, but already I was missing her. On the plane journey I had whiled away the seemingly endless hours envisaging various scenarios for the two of us – all wish-fulfilment stuff, wild fantasising in some instances. I saw us living in a beautiful thatched cottage, nestled away in the heart of the Cotswolds, Liana in her studio turning out saleable masterpieces, I in the study churning out literary bestsellers. We would have a beautiful garden (that, being an English fantasy, was green, glorious and required no attention whatsoever) in which we would frolic during the long, hot summers. We would have friends over for dinner parties – writers, artists, people from the theatre and television, as well as dear old friends from school and university days. During the winters we would take long holidays to exotic locations and bask beneath a tropical sun, returning only to the crispest of wintry days, with snow-covered fields and bright blue skies. We would huddle together on a soft rug in front of the open log fire and drink expensive cognac. We would make love by candlelight and count our myriad blessings. It would be, I knew, a perfect life.

By the time I had reached the phone box the skies had grown dark and the first few spots of rain fell on to my bare arms – I was still dressed for India – and the coldness sent a shiver up my spine. The mix of nerves and anticipation, along with my general tiredness, caused me to dial the wrong number no less than three times, but on the fourth attempt a woman answered the phone with a very polite, "Four seven six four", and I knew I was through to Liana's home.

'Is that Mrs Rogers?' I asked as politely as possible.

'Speaking.'

'I'm sorry to trouble you, but would it be possible to speak to Liana?' There was a moment's hesitation. I wasn't quite sure what Mrs Rogers said next, although I believe it was:

'She's not in at the moment. Can I take a message?'

I was, to say the least, disappointed that Liana was out; I hadn't expected there to be any delay in restarting our relationship.

'Could you tell her that Michael phoned – she has my number – and if she gets home before, say, midnight, could you ask her to call me?'

I wandered back to the house in the light rain, suddenly very weary with all that had happened. My enthusiasm and expectations had kept me going until then, but now I realised just how tired and jetlagged I was. Still, at least Liana was home, safe and sound, and it would be just a matter of hours before I'd hear from her.

I spent the rest of the evening talking to my parents about India and my experiences there. I told them about Liana, without going into any details, and mentioned that she might phone sometime.

By ten o'clock I was fighting to stay awake. Liana hadn't called, and even if she were to it was unlikely that I'd be capable of intelligent conversation, so I decided to turn in. Mum and Dad would be staying up, so if Liana phoned they were to explain that I'd gone to bed and would talk to her in the morning.

As soon as my head hit the pillow I fell into a deep,

dreamless sleep, and did not wake until ten the next morning.

With all the travelling and time changes I'd experienced in the previous few days, I had completely lost track of what day it was, so when I finally descended the stairs, heavy-lidded and dry-mouthed, I was a bit surprised to find my father sitting in the kitchen with a half-filled coffee cup, reading the papers.

'Good morning,' he said chirpily. 'How did you sleep?'
'With a vengeance,' I said. 'What are you doing here?'
He smiled. 'I live here.'
Always the joker. 'No work?'
'It's Saturday, Michael.'
'Oh,' I muttered. My head still felt thick with sleep. I slumped on to a chair, hoping someone would appear to offer me sustenance.
'Coffee?' said Dad, as if he'd read my mind.
'Please.'
'Coming up. You must still be exhausted.'
'I do feel a bit dozy. By the way, did anyone phone last night?'
Dad shook his head. 'Mum and I were up until midnight, but no one rang. Perhaps your friend didn't get home until late.'
I nodded. It seemed a perfectly reasonable explanation, but somehow I didn't feel completely happy about it.
The coffee worked wonders, and by eleven o'clock I was beginning to feel vaguely human again. I showered, dressed, and then made the first of several abortive

attempts to phone Liana. On each occasion the line was engaged, and by one o'clock I was so frustrated at not being able to speak to her that I decided to go down to Surrey and call on her in person. I could not understand why she hadn't tried to call. Even if her mother had failed to give her the message, Liana knew when I would be arriving home. I wasn't sure whether I should be worried or angry, and it was only as I left the house that I realised anger was an inappropriate response: Liana would not have forgotten, nor deliberately chosen to remain incommunicado. There would be a simple explanation, I was sure. There had to be.

It took rather longer to get to Godalming than expected and, as I was totally unfamiliar with the town, I decided to take a taxi to the address Liana had given me. The driver was familiar with Lisburn Crescent, and twenty minutes later I was standing outside number seventeen, a rather impressive Georgian house with a huge, manicured front lawn and neatly trimmed hedges. As I strode up the gravel driveway to the front door I couldn't help but smile: Liana hadn't mentioned that her family was so ostentatiously well-to-do.

I was nervous with anticipation as I rang the doorbell. I suddenly had doubts about the propriety of turning up unannounced. Perhaps I should have tried to call from the station, at least to warn the occupants that I was on my way?

I did not have much time to concern myself with such thoughts, as at that moment the door was opened by a very attractive young woman. She had shoulder-length dark hair, deep brown eyes, full, rather sensual lips. She was wearing a white sweatshirt and tight blue jeans which revealed a very pleasing shape. I noticed that she was barefoot.

'Ah, hello,' I said a little uncertainly. 'Is this the Rogers' household?' It sounded ridiculous talking this way, and I felt sure the pretty young woman would mistake me for a Seventh Day Adventist or one of those meddlesome opinion poll takers.

The woman said nothing for a moment, although her eyes gave away her evident amusement. She nodded.

'Ah, good. Erm . . . is Liana at home?'

Her expression changed then from amusement to puzzlement.

'I'm Liana Rogers,' said the girl. 'What can I do for you?'

29

Richard laughed at me the first time I mentioned fidelity to him.

'What!' he shrieked. 'Are you serious?' This is the twentieth century, Michael. Fidelity went out with Queen Victoria. No one remains faithful any more.'

'I do.'

'Then you're a fool. You're also probably in a minority of one. I mean, what's the point? There are all these gorgeous women out there, and you're restricting yourself to just one. Don't you think that's a little selfish, Michael, denying them all a chance to become intimate with you, all because of an outmoded sense of misplaced loyalty?'

'No, of course not. I think it would be unfair to Jo if I was to screw around behind her back.'

'Did I say anything about screwing around behind Jo's back? Haven't you heard of open relationships?'

'But I couldn't stand the idea of someone sleeping with Jo.'

'That,' said Richard, 'is because you're possessive. And

you're possessive because you're insecure.'

'Perhaps...'

'No "perhaps" about it. What are you afraid of Michael? That she's going to find someone who's better in bed than you are and leave you? Think about it. If she's really that fickle, she's not worth having. And if she isn't that fickle, then no harm's been done. You both get to stay together, and you both get a chance to spice up your lives a little. Could do wonders for your sex life. I mean, weren't you two both virgins when you first slept together?'

'So?'

'Well, put it this way. I could introduce you to a woman who could teach you a few things that, at present, I should imagine you could only dream of. Does Jo give a decent blow job?'

'Richard!'

'Sorry, didn't mean to get personal, it's just that... well, you could probably do with a bit of variety.'

'You're missing the point, Richard.'

'And you're missing a whole lot more. Take it from one who knows. Fidelity is just a trap, a guilt trap, devised by women to hold men back. And once they've trapped you, that's it. They start to lose respect for you; they see you as weak, ineffectual, unmanly. And before you know it, they're dropping their knickers for the first Tom, Dick or Harry who comes along with a decent chat-up line. Especially Dick.'

'That's a pretty cynical outlook.'

'Realistic, Michael, just realistic. Look, you don't owe

Jo anything. You're good to her, you're kind, you tell her you love her. None of that has to change.'

I sighed loudly. 'You don't understand, do you? I don't *want* to screw around. I don't want to be unfaithful. I don't want another woman.'

Richard stared at me blankly. 'In which case Michael, you need to see a doctor, because what you've just said is not the reaction of a normal, healthy male. Either you're sick . . . or you're lying.'

I was hurt by his accusation, which seemed designed deliberately to wound. What made it all the more hurtful was the knowledge that he'd once tried it on with Jo himself. My anger rose to the surface.

'You have no respect for anyone else's beliefs, do you? You really don't care how much you hurt people with your monomaniacal behaviour and selfishness. As long as you're happy, as long as you're having a good time, the rest of the world can go to hell.' I spat the words out at him as if they were watermelon pips, or bits of broken tooth. 'You're just an arrogant, egocentric bastard, Richard. You just don't care, do you?'

Richard stared back at me impassively. 'No,' he said. 'I don't. And you can keep on spouting your holier-than-thou attitudes and beating your chest and putting on the martyr act as long as you like, and you can be as miserable and self-righteous as you want, but answer me this, Michael. Which of us is the fool?'

There is such a thing as being too proud, and it does not necessarily take a child to point out the truth, but when Richard said these words to me, I suddenly realised that, like the Emperor, I had wrapped myself up in illusory clothes, believing myself right and true; thinking I had covered all angles, that everyone else believed the same as I; when in actual fact I was standing on a podium in full view of the world, stark naked with my dick hanging out for all to see, and only Richard had the courage to point a finger and laugh.

30

We stood staring at each other in silence for what felt like an age. I was extremely confused; for a moment I thought this might be an elaborate practical joke, but that wasn't Liana's way. Eventually the girl spoke.

'Do I know you . . . wait a moment, is your name Michael? I mean, was it you who phoned last night?'

'Yes . . .'

'Mum gave me the message, but I didn't know who it could be . . . we don't know each other, do we? I mean, have we met or something?'

I shook my head. 'Is this some sort of joke?'

The girl looked even more bemused. 'I might well ask you the same thing.' Her expression turned to one of suspicion, still tinged with a mocking wariness, as if she wasn't quite sure whether or not to act seriously. 'What do you want exactly?'

I smiled. If she was putting on an act, she was doing it with great skill. I took a deep breath. 'I'm looking for a woman called Liana Rogers. We met in India. Just forty-eight hours ago I saw her on to a plane heading back to

London. She gave me this address as her home address...' I took out the piece of paper on which Liana had scribbled the address and phone number, and showed it to the girl.

'Liana,' she said, dryly. 'That's not my name. My name's Lee. Lee Anna Rogers. I think someone *is* playing a joke on you.'

Any potential for fun and amusement seemed to fade from that point on. I felt something stick into my stomach; not a sharp pain, but a dull, heavy ache, as if I'd been kicked. 'But that's impossible... she wouldn't do that...' I was mumbling, and the girl looked at me with what appeared to be concern. I was now more confused than ever. More to the point, the poor girl in front of me evidently didn't have a clue what I was talking about. She kept staring at the paper; she seemed lost in thought.

'You're not winding me up?' she said at last.

'No, I... I know this must all seem ridiculous to you, but I swear, it's the truth. This is the address Liana gave me...'

The girl suddenly put her fingertips to her lips and looked away. 'Wait a moment,' she said, then disappeared down the hallway.

I stood there on the front porch wondering what the hell was going on. I couldn't help but think this was all some elaborate ruse designed for God-knows-what purpose. If it was a joke, I wasn't finding it the least bit funny. And if it wasn't...

The questions came thick and fast. Where was Liana?

Why had she given me this address? And what about this "Lee Anna"? It was all too bizarre, too confusing.

While I was mulling over all this in my head, desperate for some enlightenment, something that would make sense of the situation, Lee returned. In her hand was a photograph. She had a troubled expression on her face.

'The handwriting looked vaguely familiar,' she said, handing me the photograph.

'That's her. That's Liana.' It was a photograph of Liana, taken some time ago – perhaps three or four years – it was difficult to say. Her hair was longer, and she had a definite "schoolgirl" look to her. But there was no doubt. I looked up at Lee, and saw that her expression had not changed. 'What's going on?'

'You're sure that's the girl you met in India?'

'Of course . . . look, would you please tell me what's going on?'

Lee sighed. 'Her name's Angela. Angela Jane Rogers. She's my sister. And we haven't seen her for three years . . .'

31

Part of Rachel's work as a psychoanalyst involves working with the bereaved, helping them overcome their loss. She specialises in helping parents who have lost a child. These are, she says, the most heartbreaking, desperate cases that she has to deal with. To lose a loved one is tragic; to lose a child is somehow doubly so; all that potential, all that *life*, gone. She says that, on many occasions, she has been close to breaking down herself, especially when the parents are young, when it's the first child, and when a sense of responsibility or guilt enters the equation. One family had been involved in a car crash, a collision with a juggernaut on the M6. Miraculously, both mother and father had survived, although the mother had lost the use of one eye and had been laid up in hospital for several months. The child, just six years old – their only son – had been sitting in the back, and unlike the parents had not been wearing a seat belt. They both held themselves responsible for the boy's death, and it had taken two years of counselling before they could come to terms with the loss.

When Rachel told me stories such as these, something inside me would shrivel up and die, as if I could, for just an instant, understand empathically the loss these people suffered. I did not understand, however, how Rachel could cope with listening to such tragic tales day in, day out. Surely, I said, enduring a constant stream of nothing but misfortune and calamity would sour one's world view. Didn't she ever feel that the world was made up of nothing but anguish and misery? After a day of counselling, didn't she feel that there was no justice in the universe, that it was all just a haphazard jumble, a sick cosmic joke?

Rachel usually said that, no, she didn't come away from her patients feeling that way, that after a while she could distance herself from the personal feelings; that in her professional capacity, whilst she must have compassion (which necessitated a certain empathic response), if she suffered as well, she would be of no use to the poor grieving parents.

There was one occasion, however, when she had been unable to stop herself from becoming drawn into the grief. A young, single mother had been referred to her following two years of unsuccessful counselling with another analyst. The young woman's predicament was unique in Rachel's experience, and three years after the event she was still suffering from a traumatic response. One day the woman had gone, as usual, to collect her child from school. The little girl was not standing by the school gates as she had always done. She was not in the school buildings or the playground, or wandering the nearby streets. She had not gone home with a schoolfriend, no one had seen her leave the school. She was never found.

The woman could find no peace. If a body had been discovered it would have been easier for her, but the fact that she could never rest, could never know whether or not her child was alive or dead, haunted every waking hour. Everywhere she turned she would see the face of her missing child. She would wander the streets searching for her, unable to accept that the girl had gone. She had suffered numerous nervous breakdowns, and by the time she started seeing Rachel she was a wreck, a pale, pathetic shadow, unable to face the day without a tranquilliser, unable to sleep without barbiturates. She suffered constant hangovers from the sleeping tablets. She was continually ill, and had been dismissed from a string of jobs because she was unable to fulfil her responsibilities or carry out her duties. Not knowing was killing her. She had reached the stage where she actually wished that the child was dead, that there was proof, that her body had been discovered. She chastised herself for such feelings, hated herself, but said that, until she knew for sure that her little girl no longer existed, her life was nothing better than a living nightmare, a nightmare without release.

It was only after six months that Rachel realised why the woman had been referred to her. It wasn't that she was not making any progress with the previous analyst, but that the previous analyst could no longer cope with the unrelenting torment of the woman's life. Rachel found herself leaving work in tears; she would wake sometimes in the middle of the night, and her first thoughts would be of this poor woman, doomed to spend her life in a cruel twilight zone where the only release would be the news that her child, her only child, was dead. Unless, of course, her unrelenting waiting game was interrupted by her own demise.

A little knowledge, said Rachel, might be a dangerous thing, but no knowledge at all was, in some instances, the greatest curse of all. There was nothing she could do for her, and eventually she had had no choice but request that the case be taken off her hands. It was the first and only time she had made such a request.

Rachel says that she will never have a child of her own. Never.

32

'I think you'd better come in.'

Shell-shocked, I followed Lee down the hallway and into a large, spacious living room. Lee signalled to me to sit down on the sofa, while she sat in a large, over-stuffed armchair. She perched on the edge, reached for a packet of cigarettes that was lying on the coffee table, lit up and then, as an afterthought, offered me one. I had decided whilst I was flying home that I would stop smoking, but I was now so anxious that I took the proffered cigarette. I still could not quite believe that this wasn't some sort of masquerade, that I wasn't being set up. A million questions flooded into the front of my mind, but before I could get a chance to ask any of them, Lee began speaking.

'What was she doing in India? How was she? I mean, was she okay?'

'She was fine . . . but hang on Lee, are you saying that you haven't seen Liana – Angela – for three years? That she doesn't live here any more?'

'Angela hasn't lived here since 1976. There was a

big bust-up – a family row – and she just walked out.'

'Where did she go? I mean, where does she live now?'

'I don't know.'

'But you must have tried to find her, surely?'

'Yes of course. We didn't believe she was seriously leaving us. At first we thought it was just for effect; she had a tendency to be somewhat histrionic at times. But the next day when she hadn't come home, we started to worry. I phoned round all her friends, but none of them knew where she was. We tried relatives, acquaintances, anyone we could think of. Eventually Daddy contacted the police, but they seemed reluctant to help – apparently this sort of thing happens all the time. After a week, she phoned to say that she was never coming home. We pleaded with her to reconsider, but she seemed quite adamant. Mummy was beside herself with worry. I tried talking to Angela, but there was nothing I could say that would make her change her mind. It all seemed absurd – way over the top – but whatever it was that had happened had obviously affected her more deeply than any of us could have imagined. She refused to tell us where she was staying or what she was doing. She said that if any of us made any attempt to find her or bring her back, we'd be sorry. It was a genuine threat. Daddy was going to hire a private investigation firm – I didn't even know such things existed in this country – but the two or three we approached said that it would be a waste of time and money. They all said the same thing: give it a few weeks; when she was cold, hungry and tired, she'd come back.'

'She didn't?'

'No. The weeks passed and there was no contact. In the meantime we discovered that a number of valuables had been taken; some of Mum's jewellery, a pair of silver candlesticks, some rare first editions from Daddy's library. By selling that lot, plus the money she had saved from her allowance, she would have been able to look after herself for quite some time.'

'How old was she then?'

'Eighteen. She'd just left school and was due to go to university at the end of the summer... in fact, that's what the row was about. Somewhere along the line Angela had changed her mind about university. Actually, what she claimed was that she had been forced into applying by Mum and Dad, and that she had suddenly realised that she didn't want to study law at all...'

'Law? She told me she studied fine art at Kent.'

Lee nodded sadly. 'Figures. She'd always wanted to pursue art, but Mum and Dad thought she'd have a better chance in life if she studied something more vocational. She had a really good mind – she was far more intelligent than me – but she didn't care much for "practical" matters, as she put it. She loved to paint and draw, and she had some talent too, but Mum and Dad persuaded her to apply for a law degree. It was only afterwards that all the resentment came out. Angela came home one day saying that there was no way she was going to study law, even though she'd secured a place at Sussex, and if she couldn't do what she wanted, then she wouldn't go to university at all. Mum and Dad were very upset; they claimed that her mind had been poisoned, that she'd been influenced by one or other of her "hippie boyfriends" as Mum used to call them. But all Angela would say was that she'd made up her mind. There was a terrible fight that seemed to last all day. At one point she turned on me; what sort of sister was I who wouldn't support her at a time like this? I tried to keep a low profile, but Angela wanted to drag me into the fray. I didn't think I was in a position to say anything much; besides, we didn't get on all that well. There's only fifteen months between us and Angela always believed that as I was the eldest, I'd been given free reign to do as I pleased. She thought I was Mum and Dad's favourite. It wasn't that way at all, it was just that, whereas I got on with them, Angela was always battling with them. She was convinced that Mum hated her – they were always arguing about something – and that neither of them ever approved of anything she did. She saw me as Miss Goody-two-shoes, and often made me feel guilty, simply because my relationship with Mum and Dad was much less trying. There was more than a little envy – quite uncalled for. Angela was smarter, more attractive, more talented and a good deal more popular – especially with the boys – than I ever was. Anyway, the argument just got more and more heated. Suddenly, without any warning, she rushed up to her bedroom, packed a bag, and stormed off. She must have known what was going to happen and prepared everything in advance, including stashing away the jewellery and the books. It was awful.'

'So where is she now?'

'You tell me. You saw her last.'

'You mean you don't know where she lives or anything? You haven't seen her since then?'

'Well, that's not strictly speaking true. I did meet up with her about eighteen months ago. It was just a brief meeting in a café. She wrote to me at university – it was my final year – saying she desperately needed to see me. It was all very cloak-and-dagger. I was to come alone, I wasn't to tell Mum and Dad, all that sort of thing.'

'What did she want?'

'Money. She was in some sort of trouble – she wouldn't say what exactly, although I gather it had something to do with the man she was living with . . .'

'She was living with someone?'

'From what I could gather, yes. I wasn't allowed to ask too many questions. It was a dreadful meeting; Angela looked terrible – thin, grubby, pale – and I begged her to contact Mum and Dad. I told her there'd be no retribution, that they'd help her in any way they could, that they still loved her, but all she did was sneer. She was like a complete stranger to me. Anyway, I gave her a hundred pounds – that's all I could afford, and even that was stretching things a bit – and promised her I'd say nothing to Mum and Dad. We've had no contact since.'

'Where did this all take place? In London?'

'Uh-huh.'

'She didn't go to Kent then?'

'What, to university you mean? No. As far as I could

tell at that time she was living in a squat somewhere in North London, but she wouldn't say where. As to how she was getting by, I couldn't tell you. I don't think she had work, – certainly nothing above board – and to be honest, I didn't want to think about it too much. The thought of what she might be up to only upset me.'

'I can't believe this – any of this!'

Lee reached across and put her hand on my arm. 'What was she doing in India, Michael? How did you meet? How well do you know her? I can tell you're very fond of her, but . . . tell me how she is.'

I told Lee the whole story; how we met, that we had become involved, that I was in love with her. I left out the episodes concerning Liana's bizarre outbursts, but explained about her sudden change of heart with regard to travelling, and how we had decided to return home. I also related what Liana had told me of her background. Lee sat quietly through most of this, although every now and then she would shake her head as if to say, "No, that's not true either". There was no younger brother, no friend Anne, no university life. Lee herself, of course, had never been mentioned.

It wasn't until I had all but finished telling her everything that I realised how angry I had become. At some point I had risen to my feet and begun pacing around the room. I had become oblivious to my surroundings, caught up in trying to make sense of what I had been told. It was only just dawning on me that Liana had gone, disappeared, and that I had no idea where she was. These unhappy realisations interfered with my train of thought, and I found myself breaking off half-way through a sentence or just swearing out loud as the truth slowly sank in.

I tried telling Lee about the last few days in Benares, about how happy Liana had been about returning home, but it was becoming increasingly more difficult to talk coherently. By this point I was virtually shouting, each sentence peppered with choice curses of the sort I would not usually use in front of my closest friends, let alone a complete stranger. This must have been terribly embarrassing for Lee, but she said nothing and continued to listen attentively. As my anger intensified I began to babble; I knew I wasn't making sense any more, but it didn't seem to matter. Words began to pour out now in a ceaseless torrent; bits of story, half-formulated questions, ill-considered profanities.

It was absurd, but I had lost all control of what I was saying. I knew I should not be behaving this way in front of Lee, but I could not help myself. Once again, a sense of helplessness overwhelmed me as I became aware that I was out of my depth, struggling to understand what was happening.

Throughout this Lee remained silent; she seemed to understand what I was going through, or at least realised that I was not in full command of what I was saying. Eventually the words dried up and, fatigued by my outburst, I sat down once more on the sofa and closed my eyes. I was too tired and too embarrassed to look at Lee; I wanted to let her know that I wasn't some kind of nutter, that I wasn't about to do anything dangerous or frightening, but I didn't have the will. So I just sat there with my eyes closed, exhausted and on the verge of tears, wishing that someone or something would come along there and then to make everything better.

And in a strange way, it did. Because after a moment or two, I felt the gentle pressure of Lee's hand on mine, and when I opened my eyes, she was sitting beside me, nodding slowly. I knew then that I did not have to explain anything to her.

Having established that I was all right she went off to the kitchen and came back a few minutes later with two mugs of coffee.

'I don't know what to say to you, Michael. I've no idea where Angela is. I don't know how long she's been calling herself Liana or why. I don't know what she was doing in India, or how she managed to get the money to go there. I don't know why she gave you this address, and I don't know why she didn't contact you. From what you say, the two of you became very close. But you must realise, Michael, that she was never the easiest or most well-balanced of people. There was always a rebellious, slightly wild streak in her, and without knowing what's happened to her in the last few years, there's no way of knowing what she's up to or why. If I could help you, I would, but . . .' Her voice trailed off into nothingness.

I tried to piece together the spurious bits of information that Lee had given me. I thought back over the last month, searching for clues, but nothing gelled, nothing made sense. The most beautiful woman I had ever met, a woman that I was profoundly in love with, who I believed was in love with me, had walked out of my life as suddenly and mysteriously as she had arrived, and all she had left behind was a trail of question marks.

33

The last time I went down to The Sanctuary – nearly six months ago – to pick up Liana and bring her back to London, one of the staff, Doctor Jerome, took me to one side and asked to speak with me. Jerome is a very charming chap, intelligent and caring, and I'm always pleased to talk with him as he seems to take a particular interest in Liana. He is always encouraging her to paint more and, I seem to recall, he even bought one of her pieces a couple of years ago. Jerome believes, like myself, that it's good for Liana to live in London part of the year, although he thinks the pressure this places me under is injurious to my health, and would rather it was only three months instead of six. Like I said, he has a caring nature.

On this occasion he invited me into his office, sat me down with a mug of tea and asked about my most recent travels. I had, in fact, just returned from Nepal, so I entertained him with a few stories about trekking in the Himalayas and getting busted in Kathmandu. Jerome has never travelled outside Europe, and like so many people I meet, would love to visit Asia; so I haven't the heart to tell him that it's not all it's cracked up to be. I'd rather lie than destroy someone's dreams (and put myself out of a job). We chatted amiably for a while, and when I asked about Liana, the good doctor informed me that all was well, but he was a bit concerned about one thing. Apparently Liana had spent several weeks with her sketch pad making what she called "preliminary drawings" for a large watercolour, which never materialised. There was nothing particularly unusual about that; Liana often failed to follow through her initial ideas. However, what surprised Doctor Jerome was that, instead of keeping these initial drawings as she normally did, they were discovered, ripped up, in a waste paper bin. Jerome was disturbed by this as it was quite out of character. He took the shredded drawings and taped them back together again. No mean feat, he explained; a bit like doing half a dozen jigsaw puzzles, when all the pieces had been jumbled together and there were no guide pictures. Why had he bothered? I asked. He wasn't sure, all he knew was that Liana never destroyed her own work; even partially completed pieces — scribbles, sketches, cartoons — had some value to her, and she always kept them. When he had finished reconstructing Liana's pictures, he was even more disturbed. He asked if I'd mind taking a look at the sketches.

There were six pictures altogether, all done in pencil on white cartridge. Jerome had done a fine job of putting the pieces back together, and I could see it must have taken him hours.

The first picture was a self-portrait — at least, that's

what I would have called it – although it was unlike anything of Liana's I had seen previously. Liana's image stared straight out of the plane of the paper, full-face. She had managed to capture that wondrous line of her cheekbones, those clear, almond-shaped eyes, her pretty, pert nose. It was a good likeness in all respects, save one; the face was divided straight down the centre, as if cloven in two by an axe; the two parts were separated by a distance of just a quarter of an inch. It was most odd.

The second picture was rather more of a caricature, and showed a family scene; Liana's family. Her sister Lee was standing on a pedestal to the left of the picture, decked out with wings and a halo. The parents were shown kneeling before Lee, her mother in a grovelling position, her father standing. The depiction of Liana's father was particularly cruel, as the man was standing with his trousers around his ankles, clutching hold of his shrivelled penis, his tongue hanging out. He was also sporting a long tail and a pair of nascent horns which sprouted from his forehead. In the far left hand corner, gagged and bound, was Liana. The setting was recognisably the family home. This was the least elegant and subtle of all the pictures, and had evidently been executed very swiftly and in some anger.

The third picture also had something of a cartoon-like quality about it, although rather more care had been taken with it. It showed a grown man with a beard and long hair, imprisoned inside a giant bottle of Scotch. He was bashing his fists against the inside of the glass, his expression pained, the liquid reaching up to his lower lip.

The fourth picture was of the same man, a side-on view this time. The man was completely naked and fully erect, and his arms were reaching outside the frame of the picture, as if he were grasping something out of view. His face was contorted in a violent sneer. In many ways, this was the most disturbing of the pictures, as it seemed to ask many questions and left much unsaid.

The fifth picture was of a very pretty, but extremely sad little girl, sitting alone in a huge, bare room. There were bars on the window, and no visible doors. It was a desperately sad vision; it was also, of course, a self-portrait of Liana as a child, although, as I discovered shortly afterwards, Doctor Jerome had not realised this.

The final picture was a perspective drawing of a quiet road leading away into the distance. On either side of the road were hedgerows which seemed to obscure various activities which were impossible to discern. On the far horizon a range of mountains paraded across the page, and in the right foreground was the artist's own hand holding a pencil. Half-way down the road was a man, walking away. Although his back was towards us, he had turned his head to peer over his shoulder. He was carrying a shoulder bag and a camera, and he was waving goodbye. The man, of course, was yours truly.

Having studied the pictures for a while, Doctor Jerome asked me for my opinions. They were all very revealing; some more evidently so than others; it did not take a man versed in Freud and Jung to work out what the family scene was all about. But did I know the identity of the man in the bottle? What about the little girl? And the last picture; any thoughts?

I helped him as best I could. I explained that the little girl was Liana, that it was me in the final picture, and I told him about the man in the bottle and the fourth picture. As to anything else, why didn't he ask Liana? The doctor shook his head; no, he couldn't do that; it would be a betrayal of trust. After all, Liana had thrown these drawings away; he was probably not meant to see them at all.

He thanked me for my time, and made me promise not to say anything to Liana about the pictures as it would only upset her. I asked if it would be possible to have some photocopies made, as I'd rather like to look them over in more detail. He was a little reluctant at first, but once I had sworn to keep them safely locked away, he agreed.

I still have those pictures. I take them out every now and then, when Liana's not around, and study them for hours. In many ways, it is only when I look at those six snatches of Liana's soul that I understand her and her dreadful torment. For hidden in those pictures is the whole of Liana's terror . . . the whole of her life.

34

I spent the rest of the afternoon with Lee. She was immensely understanding and went out of her way to raise my spirits. As I was little more than a stranger, I thought this especially kind of her.

Lee was like her sister in many ways; her self-deprecating comments about being less attractive and intelligent seemed misplaced, and even in my distress I could not help but be drawn to her in some way. She made me promise faithfully that I would get in touch if and when Liana/Angela called. For the meantime, there seemed to be nothing I could do; I had no leads, no way of finding out where she had gone to after she had arrived back in London. Whatever I was going to do, I knew I couldn't take up any more of Lee's time. Just before I left I gave her my phone number and asked her to call me if she heard anything.

It was a long, lonely trip back, and by the time I arrived home it was dark. Winter had arrived, and the days were getting progressively shorter. A few days earlier I had been happy and in love; I had been travelling in hot, sunny, exotic India without a care in the world, and the future had looked bright and exciting. Now I was lost and lonely, stuck in the cold and dark of miserable London town, without a job, money, or place of my own. The love of my life had disappeared, and I had no idea how I would find her. It was an iniquitous state of affairs, made all the more unjust by the fact that I had no one to turn to for assistance, no right of appeal, and no one to blame except, perhaps, myself.

It must have taken a few hours for the truth to sink in, because later that night, whilst watching television with my folks, the full realisation of my predicament hit me, and I suddenly broke down. The anxiety that I had first felt at Lee's had started to fester like some rotting piece of meat. I had tried to keep a lid on it, but it was no use, and out of the blue I started to curse and yell. My parents must have thought I'd flipped. I stood up and ranted nonsensically for a few moments, then, in a great effort of will, apologised and assured them there was nothing to worry about. Rather than try to explain what was going on inside my poor confused little mind, I just ran up the stairs and locked myself in my room, where I buried my head beneath a pillow and tried to imagine that none of this was really happening, that it was all a figment of my imagination.

It didn't work.

Mum and Dad were understandably disturbed, but knew better than to question me too closely. Still, they showed great concern and later that evening Mum, displaying her usual tact, knocked gently on the door, asked if there was any way in which they might help, and casually suggested I contact one of my friends, in the hope, presumably, that someone else close to me might be able to help.

I had nothing to lose. Even though it was Saturday night I managed to get hold of Richard, who was on his way to a party. He was surprised that I was back in England, and made a couple of cracks about how he'd expected never to see me again, certain that I'd end up in some loony religious sect. This aside, he sounded pleased to hear from me, and even though it was already past ten o'clock, I arranged to meet him for a quick drink before closing time at a nearby pub in Islington.

The pub was noisy and crowded, and it took a couple of minutes before I located Richard, who was propping up the bar with a pint in one hand and a gorgeous looking blonde in the other.

'Michael! Welcome home. What are you having, usual?'

'Please.'

'It's good to see you, pal. By the way, this is Mandy. Mandy, meet Michael, my best mate. He's just come back from India; he was out there for two months, researching the effects of curried vegetables on male sexual potency.'

'Really?' said Mandy, not a hint of irony or disbelief in her voice. She was built like a model, but obviously had the brains of a stuffed toy.

'Err, not exactly . . . easy on the Dry, Richard . . .'

'It's a double.'

'Oh, right. Well, thanks.'

Mandy eyed me up and down, while Richard handed me the drink. I didn't know where Richard found these women, but they were all, I was sure, cast from the same mould. 'I've always wanted to go to India,' she said unconvincingly. 'What's it like?'

'It's a nasty, filthy place, Mandy,' interrupted Richard, 'full of short, sex-starved darkies, isn't that right, Michael?'

'Absolutely. Look Richard, do you think we could have a word?'

'Eh?'

'I need to talk to you. I need some advice.' Richard gave me his, "Not now Michael, I'm trying to score" look, but when I insisted, he made his apologies to the bimbo, gave her a kiss on the cheek and a pinch on the arse, and followed me into a quietish corner.

'I hope this is important, Michael . . .'

'She'll keep. This won't.'

Richard sat down beside me, took out his cigarettes, offered me one then lit up. 'What's up then? Catch something nasty out there?'

'Be serious a moment, will you? I've got a problem.' As briefly as I could, I outlined my predicament. I didn't tell Richard that I was in love with Liana, as he would have walked away in disgust. Instead I stressed the fact that Liana was beautiful, a fantastic lay, and unlike anything he'd ever experienced either. I knew that would keep him interested. I went into some detail about her appearance and by the time I'd finished, even he was drooling. I explained about Lee, and recounted everything she had told me about Liana. As I said, it was all a bit brief, but I think I got the main facts across to him, plus the sense of urgency and worry that I was experiencing. At first I fully expected Richard just to dismiss the whole thing and tell me to stop wasting my time; plenty more fish in the sea, that sort of thing. But on the contrary, he was quite intrigued by the whole set-up.

'And apart from the one meeting with the sister, none of the family have seen her?'

'So Lee says . . . it doesn't make any sense; I don't understand what's happened.'

Richard shrugged, then took another sip from his drink. 'Was there anything wrong with her, Michael? You know, any weird behaviour?'

'What do you mean?'

'Oh come on, you know what I'm talking about. Was she big into drugs? Any strange requests in the bedroom? Anything that might point to instability?'

I paused for a moment. I hadn't wanted to go into details, but I could tell Richard was genuinely trying to help. 'Well, there was one thing.'

'Yeah?'

'She sometimes acted strangely after we'd made love. She seemed to think I was going to hit her; she'd get really upset, and terribly withdrawn. I couldn't convince her otherwise. It was a bit like being with a schizophrenic. It only happened twice . . .'

'Wait a minute. *Did* you used to rough her up a little?'

'Richard, be serious.'

'Well I don't know, do I. Different strokes and all that.'

'There was absolutely nothing violent in my behaviour towards her. I gave her no reason to think I might hurt her.'

'And you don't think she was a junkie.'

'No. She liked her booze, but that was about it. She didn't even smoke dope.'

Richard took a deep breath and stared at the table. 'You're hooked, aren't you?'

'I suppose you could say that.'

'You sure she's worth all this worry?'

'Of course I am. Look at me, Richard; would I be confiding in you if I wasn't sure?' Richard nodded a couple of times and scratched his head. He looked uncomfortable. 'You think I'm crazy, don't you?'

Richard sighed. 'I'm just looking at the facts, Michael. She's not really living in the real world, is she? She's made up some fantasy about her home life, about her family, about her friends. She told you she had a degree when she never even went to university. She also told you she was a virgin, and from what you've told me, there's no *way* she was as pure and innocent as she claimed. Besides, her sister said that she was living with someone, right?'

'She thought so, but she didn't actually know. Besides, that was eighteen months ago.'

'Well, I think it's safe to assume there's a bloke in the picture somewhere. If this woman is as mind-blowingly gorgeous as you claim, it's unlikely she'd have had three years away from home without some sort of liaison. She's also, from what you say, suffering from a quite unreasonable belief that you're going to beat her up after sex. And now she's disappeared. Now, you can check with your mate Rachel about this, but it sounds to me like this chick is both a pathological liar and a paranoid schizophrenic.'

'I haven't told you all this so that you can make a diagnosis...'

'Listen, you arsehole. All I'm saying is, no matter how beautiful this woman is, do you really want to get involved with someone who's that unbalanced? Because if the answer is yes, then you've got a number of problems on your hands. First, you have to find her. The very fact that she hasn't contacted you suggests to me that, regardless of what happened in India, she's changed her mind about being with you. There could be any number of reasons, but whatever they are it's going to be an uphill struggle. Second, just supposing you do get together, what then? How do you know she won't just walk out on you again? Third, what if there is really something wrong with this woman? Something serious, organic, whatever they call it. What if she's nuts?'

'Richard!'

'I'm just trying to point out that this isn't some sort of game, Michael, that if you intend to do anything about this, you may be letting yourself in for more than you bargained for. Finally, there may be someone else in the picture, another bloke. Now come on, Michael, do you really want all those hassles?'

I finished the Scotch and Dry. 'What I want is some help. And another drink.'

'It's your round. As for help, what can *I* do?'

'I don't know. I just thought you might have some ideas as to how I might find her.'

Richard shook his head. 'Michael, you dragged me over here to ask for some advice. And my advice is, do nothing. If she gets in touch with you, then take it from there, but for fucksake, be careful.'

'But I can't just sit around waiting for a phone call that might never come. I'll go mad.'

'What choice do you have? True enough, you can't just sit around; you have to get on with your life. Have you thought about what you're going to do? Of course not – I know you. Well, school-days are over, friend. There's no one paying your way any more; you have plenty of things to think about and keep you occupied.'

'You're not being much help.'

'What do you want from me, Michael! I can't go out searching the streets for some loony sex-goddess. And neither can you. I don't mean to be so hard, but you've got to be practical Michael. I can see she means a lot to you; if half of what you've told me is true, I can even understand it. But she's not here, is she? And she left no forwarding address, so until she decides to contact you, there's nothing more you can do. Now then, why don't you buy me a drink and after that we can head off to this party. Mandy has a few friends coming along, and some of them are corkers. They may not be Liana, but they might just take your mind off her for a while. What do you say?'

What could I say? He was right of course; there was nothing I could do, at least, nothing I could think of doing. Given the alternatives, a party seemed like the most sensible option. After all, I could always get pissed . . .

35

'Have you seen Rachel lately?'

'What are you talking about?'

'I was just wondering if you'd seen Rachel.'

'Don't be daft, Liana; you know I haven't.'

'When was the last time you saw her then?'

'I don't remember; it was ages ago . . .'

'I don't believe you, Michael. Where were you on Thursday night?'

'Please, Liana. Not now; not here.' I ordered another coffee from a passing waiter.

'You were with her, weren't you. Why won't you just tell me the truth?'

'Don't do this, Liana; I'm not in the mood.'

The restaurant had been fairly quiet for most of the evening; the food had been first class, the service acceptable, and the Sauvignon a delight. The theatre crowds had descended at about ten thirty, and now there was an energetic buzz to the place which I found appealing. I like people-watching as a rule, but most particularly in London. When I return from my six-month stint abroad, one of the first things I do is take in a play and a meal in the West End; it is also, usually, one of the last things I do before heading off again.

Liana had been on her best behaviour – I know that sounds terrible, as if she were some sort of pet that had to be watched or something – but that's what it comes down to sometimes. We had taken in an early film – the new Scorsese – which had been as good as anticipated, with De Niro turning in a bravura performance as usual, before coming on to the restaurant. It was, I suppose, a treat of sorts for both of us; we hadn't been out of the house for four or five days, and I needed a break from the typewriter. Liana had been nagging me to take her out all day. Her mood had been relatively calm, and she hadn't caused a scene for days. I was a bit unprepared, therefore, when she brought up Rachel's name. I should have realised then and there that this would lead to trouble, but the film, the meal, and the three glasses of wine had relaxed me so much that I had completely let down my guard. Absolutely fatal, as Liana can sense this like a dog picking up a scent, and she had left it until just that moment before pouncing. She's crafty like that.

'Don't give me that shit, Michael. I can tell when you're lying to me.'

'Liana, you know damn well that I haven't seen Rachel all the time you've been here.'

For reasons that have never made any sense to me, Liana is terribly jealous when it comes to Rachel. She knows that the relationship is as close to platonic as one could hope to find, but this seems to make no difference to her. Liana thinks that I'm cheating on her.

Liana affected her best sneer. 'You fucking liar,' she said, rather too loudly for comfort. The couple on the next table looked over; a big mistake. 'And you can mind you're own fucking business as well . . .'

'Liana! Waiter, the bill please . . . and if you don't behave yourself . . .'

'What? You'll put me over your knee and spank me?'

'Keep your voice down . . .'

'You'd like that, wouldn't you? A bit of macho posturing; that's a real turn on for you, all that slapping and hitting . . .'

'Shut up . . .'

' . . . you'll probably come in your underpants.'

'That's enough! Waiter, please.'

Liana stared at the couple on the next table, and addressed the woman. 'Does he slap you about? Does he? Does he threaten you with violence if you don't suck him off?'

That was it. I grabbed her firmly by the arm and dragged her away from the table. There's no reasoning with her when she gets like this. I didn't even bother apologising to the poor couple; what, after all, could I say? Liana struggled a bit, but I gripped her arm firmly.

'Ouch! Get off me you bully! Let *go*!'

The entire restaurant was looking at us now. I'm past the stage where I really give a shit what people think of me; that's the great irony. I don't care if they think I'm a molester, a violent wife-beater, whatever; they can think what they like. But I won't have them think ill of Liana. It's not her *fault*; she can't really help it. I can't just stand there and explain to fifty complete strangers that there's no need to panic, everything's okay, my wife's mad, please carry on as if nothing happened . . . and as I can't say that, I have only one option; to escape as quickly as possible. I won't have them thinking badly of Liana. They don't know her, they know *nothing* about her or what she's been through. They just don't know.

'Get your hands off me, you bastard!'

As we pushed past the cashier's desk I indicated that I'd be back in just a moment, then shoved Liana out through the door. Liana was still yelling.

'You've got no right to treat me this way!'

'Shut up. I'm going back inside to pay the bill. Now for Christ's sake, calm down. If you stop ranting I'll tell you everything you need to know, okay?'

'So it's true! I knew it . . .'

'Just stay there.'

I went back inside, apologised to the *maitre d'*, paid the bill, left an overly generous tip, then went back outside where I'd left Liana, fuming.

'I knew it, you snake,' she spat. 'You can't keep your dick to yourself, can you, you've got to go sticking it up the first tart who'll have it . . .'

'This is unnecessary, Liana. You know damn well that I . . .'

'I know damn well that you're a sneak and a liar, and that you've been screwing around behind my back!'

'I'm not prepared to get into an argument about this. Now come on, we're going home.'

'What, so you can rough me up?'

'Don't be ridiculous.' I hailed a passing taxi, bundled Liana inside, gave the address to the driver, and waited for the onslaught of abuse. Liana had stopped screeching – probably because there was no longer an audience – but she was still visibly upset.

'How can you do this to me, Michael? How can you be so cruel?'

'Liana, you're letting your imagination get the better of you.'

'But you've *lied* to me . . .'

'I haven't lied. Now listen to me. I haven't seen Rachel for over six months. I've spoken to her a few times on the phone, but that's it. Why do you insist on torturing yourself like this?'

'You're the one who's doing the torturing. You're incapable of being faithful.' She started to cry.

Like most people, I resent being accused of things that I haven't done. Liana accuses me of screwing Rachel. She has her reasons; she knows that Rachel and I are close. She finds it impossible to believe that we have not been carrying on an affair behind her back, and my protestations fall on deaf ears. This is not to say that I am not guilty of infidelity, if such a term can be used in these circumstances. There has been the occasional bout of sexual profligacy with some "bimbo" as Liana calls them. It's never led to anything serious, it's never altered my feelings for Liana and, despite the attraction of such an idea sometimes, it would never cause me to leave Liana. I'm not particularly proud of my behaviour, but I will not renounce it either. I'm a human being; I have my desires and needs like everyone else, and whilst those needs exist I will do what is necessary to fulfil them. And before you cast the first stone, be aware of one thing; Liana and I have not made love for three years. All her talk of fidelity is an irrelevance. It reached a point where I was no longer able to suffer the torments that followed lovemaking; Liana's paranoia became so far advanced that any physical relationship between us became impossible. I am not cheating on Liana; there is nothing to cheat.

'Stop crying, Liana; you're just upsetting yourself.'

'Why won't you make love to *me* . . . you used to want me . . .'

'Not again Liana; we've been through this a thousand times.'

'Why don't you love me any more?'

All this from the woman who threatens to cut my balls off if I tell her I love her.

Well, what would *you* do? Devil or deep blue sea? Let me tell you something, it isn't much of a choice. In fact, it isn't any choice at all.

As Richard would say, take it from someone who knows. Never fall in love with beauty, frailty, charisma or charm. Especially charm. Look it up in the dictionary. It's not just the quality of pleasing, fascinating or attracting people; it is also a magic spell, or the formula used in casting such a spell. Ten years ago I fell under that spell, and I've been bewitched ever since. It's made a mockery of my life. No, if you're going to fall in love, make sure it's for the right reasons: money, company, security, prestige, kudos. Better still, try not to fall in love at all. The song says it all: love hurts. Turn on the radio any time, day or night, and listen to those lyrics. For every song praising the joys of being in love, there are ten delineating the pains of lost love, broken love, love turned sour, love that walks out the door, love turned to hate. All over the world there are millions of people suffering the agonies of heartbreak. Can anything really be worth all that pain?

No, of course not. So why do we do it? Why do we do this to ourselves? Why do we fall in love? You're hoping for an answer, right?

Dream on, friends. Dream on.

36

I did not stay long at the party. There were a number of old friends there, but I was in no mood to make small talk with them; there was far too much on my mind. As for Mandy's friends, they were, true to form, attractive enough, but not even the sexiest of them could take my mind off Liana. In the end I made my apologies to Richard, told him I'd be in touch, and took a cab home.

I slept poorly that night, the dark hours beset by nightmares and disjointed images. In one sequence, I found myself walking down a local street when I saw Liana appear from a doorway. I ran towards her calling her name, but she didn't hear me, and started to walk away. I chased her down the street, yelling her name, and eventually caught up with her; I grabbed her by the arm, spun her round, and came face to face with her sister Lee, who didn't seem to recognise me at all. In another dream, I was sitting in a restaurant with Liana, drinking beer. It was a perfectly normal scenario, and in the dream I remembered thinking: what was all the fuss about? She's here. We were talking and laughing, just as we had done a dozen times or more in India. Everything seemed fine until I realised that Liana was becoming less distinct as we talked. As the conversation continued, I began to panic; she was becoming more and more insubstantial with every second. I tried to take hold of her, but my hand passed straight through her. Liana seemed totally oblivious to all of this, carrying on as if nothing was wrong. Within moments she had become totally transparent, and then, with her laugh echoing in the air around me, she vanished altogether.

When I finally woke, I was as tired as if I had had no sleep whatsoever.

I spent the rest of the day reading the Sunday papers half-heartedly, trying to formulate some sort of plan. I knew Richard was being perfectly logical when he said there was nothing I could do, but I was also aware that there was no way I could just "get on" with living my life. I knew that I would get no rest until I had made contact with Liana again.

That evening I called Lee, and asked her to help me.

'But what can I do?' she said, somewhat surprised to hear from me.

'The café where you met her; can you remember where it was?'

'Yes, it was on Charing Cross Road... I don't remember the name of the place, but I'd recognise it. Why?'

'Did she seem comfortable there; I mean, do you

suppose it was a local haunt of hers, a place she went to regularly?'

Lee paused. 'I couldn't say, Michael. It was quite a while ago, and I was so concerned about seeing Angela that I wouldn't have picked up on something like that.'

'Well, it might be worth a try. I mean, perhaps the staff know her; perhaps she still goes occasionally . . . someone might know something.'

'It's a bit of a long shot, don't you think?'

'Lee, I've nothing else to go on; I have to try. I'll go crazy just sitting around waiting.'

Lee paused. 'Well, I'll be happy to take you there. How about we have lunch there?'

'That'd be great.'

'Fine. Meet me tomorrow outside Foyles, twelve o'clock. Okay?'

'It's a date. And thank you.'

'It's okay, really; it'll be nice to see you again. Just . . . well, I don't want to sound like a wet blanket, but just for your own sake, don't get your hopes up, Michael. It may lead to nothing.

'I know. But I have to have hope, Lee. I have to.'

'Yes, of course. See you tomorrow then.'

Lee was quite right; it was very unlikely that anything would come of returning to the café, but at least I felt as if I was doing something rather than just sitting around waiting for a miracle. I slept well that night.

I woke to a crisp, bright morning, the sort of winter's

day that makes December in England a bearable experience. The winds were blowing briskly, clearing away cobwebs from every corner, and the clouds sped by as if someone had pushed the fast forward button, allowing a pale yellow sun to show through now and then and cast its anaemic shadows on the frosty ground. Even the leafless trees, shivering in their nakedness, seemed overly excited, waving their branches with a greater urgency than I'd previously noticed. A sense of anticipation was threaded through the frozen air; wisps of expectancy were already woven into the fabric of the nascent day.

As I climbed the stairs out of Tottenham Court Road station, I was gripped by a sense of mounting excitement. I was en route to a rendezvous with a beautiful stranger in order to track down her sister, my missing lover; it was like a scenario from an American movie. What would we discover? If any information were forthcoming, where would it lead us? What would we find at the end of the track? As I wandered down the Charing Cross Road, the excitement drove out my feelings of despair, if only for a few moments. One adventure – a love affair – had, almost instantly, given way to another – a mystery – and only a few elements and characters linked the two, as if I had been thrust into the sequel before I'd finished watching part one. It was a decidedly odd sensation.

Lee was waiting for me, as arranged, outside the book shop. She looked even lovelier than when I'd first seen her, and with the wind sweeping her hair back from her face, her resemblance to Liana was more apparent; she had the same fine bone structure and perfect skin, that same sexy glint in her eye. She greeted me with a kiss on the cheek.

'Hello, Michael; blowy, isn't it!'

'Just a bit; you must be freezing. Have you been waiting long?'

'Just a couple of minutes. Come on, let's get out of this hurricane; the café's just along here.'

She grabbed me by the arm and led me to the café. It was a simple but pleasant sandwich bar, run by a boisterous Italian family. It was not yet lunch-time, so the place was relatively quiet. We found a table by the window, sat opposite each other and ordered two cappuccinos and a couple of sandwiches.

'What now?' said Lee, grinning wildly.

'Are you making fun of me?'

She shook her head. 'No, not at all; why do you say that?'

'I wouldn't blame you for thinking me crazy, dragging you along on a wild goose chase like this.'

'I don't think you're crazy at all; I think this is fun . . . I mean, I know it's a serious business and all that, but . . . well, I couldn't help but feel quite excited this morning.'

I smiled. 'I know what you mean; I felt exactly the same way.' A young, dark-haired lad – about sixteen or seventeen at a guess – brought the cappuccinos. He had a certain swagger in his step, as if he was acting out some role or other, trying to be older, more mature and sophisticated than his years allowed. I thanked him deliberately; I wanted to come straight out and ask him if he knew a beautiful twenty-one-year-old woman called Liana Rogers, but it seemed an absurd thing to do. I took a deep breath, and as he left I looked across to Lee and shrugged my shoulders. Lee laughed. 'This is crazy; I don't know where to start.'

'Well, how about trying this.' Lee reached into her bag and brought out the photo of Liana that she had shown me previously.

'Smart thinking; you missed your vocation.'

'"Lee Rogers: Private Dick!" . . . I'm not sure I like the sound of it really; what do you think?'

'Let's see how we get on with this case; if it's a success, perhaps we could set up our own business.'

Lee grinned. 'I can just see it now; we'd be inundated with phone calls from little old ladies wanting to find their missing Tibbles or Poopsies . . .' She took a sip of her coffee. 'Well, go on then. See what they have to say.'

The same lad who had served our coffee came over at that moment with our sandwiches. As he placed them on the table, I took the photo and held it up to him.

'Err, look, sorry to bother you, but do you know this woman? I mean, have you seen her lately?'

The lad threw me a look, somewhere between bemusement and suspicion, then took the photo. He nodded his head.

'Nice lookin' chick,' he said, his accent betraying his origins as closer to Romford than Rome. He obviously fancied himself as a bit of a lady-killer; he was wearing very tight blue jeans, a white shirt, undone to mid-chest, and a gold chain around his neck. His hair was slicked back, and some dark, scrappy stubble was erupting from various places on his chin. The overall effect was more amusing than seductive. 'Wos the story then?' he said, the words bracketed by sniffs at either end.

I suppressed my laughter while Lee did her best to explain.

'She's my sister. She hasn't been in touch for a while, and we're a bit worried about her, that's all. I know she used to come here sometimes . . . I met her here myself. We just thought someone might know where she is.'

The kid shrugged and nodded a couple of times as if to say "fair enough" and then stared at the photo for another few moments.

'Well, I've only been workinere a coupla munfs, so I wooden know. But angabout, I'll arse Tony. Ere, Tony! Getchyarse overere.'

Tony, presumably the boy's older brother, came out from behind the counter. He must have been in his early twenties, tall and slim with a strong, attractive Italianate appearance; I caught Lee looking him up and down in a transparently sexual manner, and to my amazement felt a pang of what could only be jealousy. I pushed it aside, promising myself to examine it later on.

'What's the problem?' The photo was thrust into Tony's hands.

'These two are lookin for this chick. D'you know her?' asked the younger brother.

Tony looked up and nodded. 'Sure. It's Liana, innit.'

Lee and I looked at each other. 'When did you last see her?' asked Lee.

Tony hesitated a moment. 'She in trouble or something?'

'Thas her sister,' said the lad in mock exasperation.

'We'd just like to get in touch; does she still come here?'

Tony shook his head. 'Haven't seen her here for, what, six months probably. She used to drop in all the time. I was wondering what had happened to her myself.'

'So you've no idea where we can find her?' asked Lee.

'Nah, not really. Last thing I know she was living in a squat up in Wood Green with that dickhead boyfriend of hers.'

I felt something cold and steely grip my guts. 'Boyfriend?'

'Yea, you know, whasisname...' Tony stared into space for a moment, then looked over to the counter. 'Hey, Ma, you remember that creep always hanging around with Liana?' Mama's expression told the whole story. 'What was he called?'

'Keith,' spat Mama.

'Oh yeah, that's him. Keith.'

'I never met him,' I said. 'Why didn't you like him?'

Tony eyed me suspiciously, as if I should have known Keith, or at least known of him. 'He had this way about him; I can't say for sure. There was something very dodgy about him. For one thing, he was a real scrounger. He never had any money; whenever they came in here, it was always Liana who paid. And he had a real nasty temper. No, I just didn't like him; she was much too good for someone like him.'

'And they were living in a squat.'

'Yeah. They used to hold parties there sometimes. She invited me to one not so long ago – eight, maybe nine months – but I couldn't make it.'

My heart suddenly skipped a beat. This was it, the information we needed! 'You have her address, then?'

Tony looked at me blankly. 'Nah, afraid not. I mean, she probably gave it to me, but . . . well, it was a while ago now.'

Lee must have sensed the disappointment that all but swamped me, because she reached across the table and took hold of my hand, giving it a little squeeze.

'Are you quite sure you don't have the address?' she asked, her manner calm. Again she seemed to be giving Tony a pretty strong signal. Tony, who had evidently caught on to this by now, turned his attention directly towards her.

'I'll tell you what I'll do. I'll go check my address book. Robert,' he said to his younger brother, 'get two more cappuccinos for . . . what did you say your name was?'

'Lee; and this is Michael.'

'Okay. Come on, don't just stand there, get Lee and Michael some coffee. I'll be right back.'

Tony disappeared up some stairs at the back of the café.

'I think you have more in common with your sister than you've let on.'

'Huh?'

'I think he'd have carried you in his arms to Wood Green if you'd asked.'

Lee laughed. 'Men like that are *so* transparent; you

only have to pay a little more than cursory attention, breathe a little heavier than normal, and they think you're half-way to orgasm just by looking at them.'

'He is good-looking though.'

'Yeah, and he knows it. Good-looking men make the most selfish lovers, Michael. All that pride, vanity and self-love; there's not enough room in the bed for a woman as well.'

'Well, let's hope he was sufficiently interested in your sister to have made a note of her address.'

Tony reappeared looking less than ecstatic. 'Sorry,' he said, 'but I can't find an address. I looked in the diary, but all I found was "Liana, party, Queen's Arms after ten."'

'Is that a pub?'

'Yeah, up on Lordship Lane.'

'And that's all?'

'Yeah, sorry about that. Listen, if you do catch up with her, tell her she's welcome back here any time; I'd really like to see her again.'

I'll bet you would, I thought, but said nothing. Besides, Tony was supremely indifferent to my existence, preferring to drool over Lee instead. Once again I noted the resentment I felt at what seemed like an intrusion; was it because Lee was so like Liana that I felt sexual jealousy when I was around her?

'Thanks for your help, Tony,' I said. 'We'll let you know if we hear anything.'

'Yeah, sure,' he said, without actually acknowledging me. Then, to Lee: 'Shall I give you a call if she turns up here again?'

'Thank you, yes.' She then proceeded to give Tony *my* phone number, and shot a conspiratorial wink at me in the meantime.

We finished the sandwiches and coffee. It was not yet one, although the café was just beginning to fill. Lee grabbed her bag and stood up.

'Fancy a drink, then?'

'Don't tell me; the Queen's Arms?'

'By Jove Holmes, how did you know?'

'Elementary, my dear Watson. Elementary.'

37

There is nothing quite like falling in love. Remember the last time you fell in love? Remember the way time changed, overnight, from a smooth, unhurried continuum to a frantic, accelerated, spasmic dance, where mere seconds sometimes lasted for ever, and days would whisk past at a gallop? And those breathless phone calls and impassioned declarations; when else do you talk like that, with such devotion, such intensity? And the pledges and covenants; everlasting this, eternal that, as if love transformed us from constrained mortals to limitless superheroes, capable of anything and everything, faster than a speeding bullet, leaping tall buildings in a single bound. What is it about love that makes us so incapable of behaving like *real* people? We think of true love as a genuinely adult emotion, but inevitably it reduces us to the most fantastic phases of childhood. We pine, we cry, we have tantrums, we don't eat our food, we stop playing with our other friends, we become completely indulgent and expect everyone else to indulge us too. We make the most extravagant promises; we will lasso the moon and bring it to earth, we will climb every mountain, we will make someone happier than they have ever been in their lives, than they could possibly have imagined.

Where do we *get* these ideas from? Who do we think we are?

Ah, love. No feeling comes close to that overpowering amalgam of hope, delight, mystery, pleasure, anticipation and desire. There are few moments in our life when we connect, when we stop feeling alone, when, if only for a short while, we allow something bigger than us to overwhelm our egos, make them subservient to the whole. Is it any wonder we talk about wanting to drown in another's love, of being consumed by love? To lose that aloneness, to lose that individualness, to feel that we belong, that we are one with the world. Is this not the same experience that the great mystics and teachers describe when they speak of nirvana? Few events in our lives encompass such emotional intensity. Like the first hit of an unadulterated narcotic, when we fall in love our body chemistry energises; senses sizzle, synapses spark; we soar towards critical mass, and our whole world becomes one giant, organic reaction, heading for that supreme, irreversible melt-down.

Such is the power of these feelings, it's a wonder we don't fall in love more frequently.

Or is it? If the process of falling in love is the closest most of us get to nirvana, then falling out of love is the closest we come to hell. However, it all balances out in the long run; after all, it takes only the simplest piece of reasoning to see that, in a lifetime, one will never fall out of love more times than one falls in love, whereas the reverse may be true. I find that reducing a life to banal mathematical probabilities is one of the best ways to remain sane when your world is falling apart. There are a number of these equations which, if we but took more notice of them, would resolve many of our difficulties. For instance, with regard to the above statement, if x is the number of times we fall in love, and y the number of times we fall out of love, x will always be either equal to y, or equal to $y + 1$ (in the event that we fall in love for the final time and live happily ever after). And there are others. It is perhaps not widely known that a person's problems are directly proportional to the number of keys he/she carries around. Sceptics should note that the truth of the theory is borne out through simple observation. Also, the measure of a person's freedom is inversely proportional to the size of their phone bill. It may not be an exact science, but then neither is sociology.

When it comes to love, the only other equation that seems to hold is that, if x is the measure of your love for your partner, and y is the measure of your partner's love for you, then x will always be either greater than or less than, but will never equal y.

And one final theory — a sort of variation on the "my best friend's wife" syndrome — which merely states that one is much more likely to start an affair with one's partner's closest friend or relative than with a complete stranger. As the likelihood of infidelity is a function of the similarity between one's partner and the object of desire, twins and close siblings should be considered particularly vulnerable.

Love is so fickle, so uncertain. In a world where we all chase the highest quality, dedicate our lives to the pursuit of happiness, it seems strange that we should put so much faith in such a poor, handicapped creature like love; it is blind, it knows no rules, it has no conscience, it can make you sick, it can turn sour. We'd all be better off with maths. At least you can always count on two plus two.

Can't you?

38

It was difficult to think of Wood Green as London. Although it was only a few miles further out than my own stamping ground, there was something unremittingly suburban about the place. Even back then, Islington had a life of its own, a character, a pulse; it had, for want of a better expression, a *raison d'etre*. You walked along its streets and alleyways, and it sang out to you; not a symphony *à la* New York or Paris, nor the graceful chamber music of Venice or Florence, but at least it had a melody, a harmony, a structure. But what did Wood Green have? What sounds emanated from its shallow depths, its soulless interior, other than a sort of atonal bleating? It was odd how something so characterless and bland could also be so offensive. It wasn't that Wood Green was ugly; it just wasn't *anything*. For an individual to lack the courage of his or her convictions is sad, but for a whole town to exude nothing more than a sort of attenuated self-pity is pathetic. It did not possess a single redeeming feature, and was so dull, so insignificant, that had a bomb dropped on the high street, I don't think anyone would have noticed. And this was where Liana had lived? It was inconceivable.

The Queen's Arms was not the sort of place in which I'd have chosen to spend the early part of my afternoon, had there not been a very specific reason. I'm not very comfortable in strange pubs, especially within a city; I always feel out of place, unwelcome, as if I'm walking on to someone else's territory. It's totally irrational, especially as I'm quite prepared to walk into a completely unfamiliar bar in a totally foreign country without thinking twice about it. Ignorance of the specific social conventions that operate in a foreign country means one can behave, not so much with impunity, but certainly with abandon. However, stepping into a little-known manor can be fraught with difficulties, and to waltz into a drinking house wearing the wrong clothes or expression may be tantamount to walking naked into a church, cursing and spluttering.

London pubs are far from homogeneous entities, differing greatly from region to region; upmarket, downmarket, fancy, dirty, simple, traditional, high-tech, friendly, aggressive, cosy, noisy, vibrant, sleepy . . . you name it, you'll find it. My own personal taste runs towards the traditional/cosy, the sort of pub where the landlord knows you by name, greets you with a smile, enquires sincerely about your day/wife/dog/loft conversion before asking if you'd like your usual. The music, if there is any, will be unobtrusive, there are no nasty, noisy machines, and in general there's more wood than plastic to be seen. My local in Islington is like that, and I always feel comfortable there. In fact, the older I get, the more I've come to treasure the familiar and the comfortable, rather than seeing them as traps or the first signs of middle age complacency. Whatever, when it comes to spending time in a pub, I have always chosen the traditional/cosy, unless it's a special occasion like a birthday or celebration, in which case, a vibrant/upmarket spot with music and overpriced cocktails with daft names can be quite fun. What I would not do under normal circumstances is stay long in a noisy/dirty/aggressive/downmarket establishment like the Queen's Arms. I hadn't realised that sort of pub still existed; it made the seedy dives in and around Islington look like sumptuous palaces.

The lounge bar was virtually deserted, so we wandered into the public bar and sat at a couple of stools by the counter. Sitting by the window were a group of older men, arguing noisily and gesticulating wildly, spilling beer and chain smoking. A couple of skinheads playing pool stopped their game and their stream-of-consciousness swearing to stare at us in a manner that made it clear they were not especially pleased to have a couple of strangers in their local. We had been there less than a minute and I was ready to leave. Lee sensed my discomfort and with just a touch of her hand, calmed me down. I was struck once again by her composure and, indeed, her fine looks. Like her sister, Lee seemed not just aware of her beauty, but, unlike many beautiful women, comfortable with it, aware that others would look, stare, ogle, and that somehow it was not only understandable, but acceptable, a sort of implicit price that one must pay for having been blessed with an exquisite appearance. Lee's hand just lay there on my forearm, and she stared into my eyes, sure and certain, in complete control of herself and the situation in which we found ourselves. For a moment I felt myself slipping away, as if I was falling under a spell; there was something extraordinary about these Rogers girls, and in that moment I had a fleeting, barely tangible sense that, in one way or another, my life would be for ever inextricably linked with theirs.

The barman, a tall, greasy-haired youth with a nasty jagged scar down one cheek, eyed us suspiciously for several minutes before approaching us.

'Wodja want?'

Great, I thought, the snob in me rising reflexively; Neanderthal staff. We should get some very informative grunts out of this one. I pushed the thought away as quickly as I could; I was uncomfortable enough in the surroundings without sending out death-wish signals as well. 'Half a lager, please. Lee?'

Lee shuffled on her seat and smiled at the barman; it was exactly the same look she had given the Italian stallion in the café. There was something about this behaviour which both amused and shocked me; that Lee could be so calculating surprised me; that she was capable of pulling it off so successfully, deluding these singly transparent men with their chisel jaws and overactive glands, made me want to laugh out loud. I did not, of course, but merely sat back and allowed Lee to weave her spell.

'I'll just have an orange juice,' she purred at the barman. He made a feeble attempt to disguise what he was thinking, but frankly, if there'd been a flag attached to the end of it, it would have been waving in our faces. 'Oh, and perhaps you could help me with some information?'

'Wozzat then?'

Lee produced the photo and handed it over. The barman studied it for a moment, then looked at Lee. He narrowed his eyes, presumably in an attempt to show he was thinking intently, but, alas, merely destroying any illusion of faint intelligence that had been present previously. 'Oh, I gerrit. You Liana's sister or somefink?' Lee smiled and nodded. A broad grin spread out across the barman's face as if, against all odds, he'd just won the finals of *Mastermind*. 'Yeah, right . . . family resemblance.'

'You know where she is?' asked Lee casually.

The barman nodded, although it did not seem to signify assent. 'Actually, aven't seen erfra coupla munfs, allvo she's usually in ere awler time. Aven't seen mutcha wotsisface nyver . . .'

'Keith?'

'Yeah, Keef. Good bloke Keef, when he ain't office fuckin trolley. He did come in the uvver night, buh nofferlong.'

Lee nodded, flashed him another one of her sexy looks, then executed a nice little bluff.

'They still living round the corner then?'

'Yeah, finkso.'

'Don't suppose you can remember the address, can you?'

The barman spent the next minute doing his best impression of a man with no brain, before coming back to our planet with a decisive reply.

'Nah. Never could remember numbers... buh seasy to find. Sup the road, firs onner left, larse hass onner left... Eldon Road, I fink.'

'Of course,' said Lee, and smiled gratefully. 'Thanks. What are you having?'

'Oh, fanks very much. I'll avven arf. Cheers.'

Lee turned to me and smiled. I could have thrown my arms around her and kissed her, but knew that this was neither the time nor the place for such a demonstrative outburst.

'You're amazing,' I said quietly once the drinks had arrived.

'Just doing what comes naturally,' said Lee, in a way that aroused me more than a dozen of those looks ever could. I could almost hear my heartbeat quicken and feel my palms becoming hot and damp. This was not an acceptable reaction, I remembered thinking, and did my best to put it down to general excitement. After all, we had started the day with nothing, and we now had an address; of course I was excited. And she did look very much like her sister; it was only natural. I was only human, and just because I was profoundly in love with someone else didn't mean I wasn't allowed to find other women attractive, especially someone who bore such marked similarities to the woman I loved. There was nothing wrong with any of this; it was perfectly acceptable and understandable behaviour.

Which makes me wonder why I felt so dreadfully guilty as we left the pub and started walking towards Eldon Road.

39

I read a review in last week's *Sunday Times* of a first novel by some young, up and coming writer, whose name, at present, escapes me. The book, entitled *Mythopoeia* and referred to as "a literary, post-modernist romance" (whatever that is), was praised for its ingenuity and the unique manner in which a particular genre (the romance, usually considered undistinguished as an art form) was given a new lease of life by the young author. In the same breath, however, the novel was severely criticised for its poor character development. In fact, the reviewer went to great lengths, selecting various passages by way of example, to show that a number of key figures in the novel frequently behaved "out of character". The reviewer went so far as to suggest that this inconsistency was responsible for the ultimate failure of what was otherwise "a fine first attempt", but he was sufficiently generous (and condescending) to suggest that such failings were merely the product of the author's extreme youth and immaturity, and that we might still look forward to a fine novel from the young whippersnapper once he had grown up.

Now then, I'm not a great reader. (I tend to go for those mindless airport novels when I'm travelling as they require no effort to read, are instantly forgettable, and are great for swatting mosquitoes and hurling at cockroaches. Besides, great novels, important novels, depress me. They're a taunt, a constant reminder that I'm just an ordinary wordsmith, a hack.) However, I was so infuriated by this particular reviewer's attitude that, against my usual nature (that is, acting out of character) I went out and purchased, in hardback no less, a copy of *Mythopoeia*.

It was only two hundred pages or so in length and I managed to read the entire book in two sittings. I confess it was, at times, a little too intellectual for my taste, a bit self-conscious and, perhaps, a little too clever for its own good, but there was one aspect of the book that was simply breath-taking in its execution. You've probably guessed it.

The characters in *Mythopoeia* were drawn with such care, such insight, such astonishing perspicacity, that they were not fictions at all; they were real. They did not act or speak or behave like characters in any other novel I had ever read. They were not rational. They were not consistent. They did not, in each case, "develop" or "progress" during the course of the novel. They were full of idiosyncrasies, capable of inexplicable behaviour and outrageous acts. They were, mostly, confused, both by their own actions and the actions of other characters. Attempts by one or other to understand instances of bizarre behaviour invariably came to nothing. Questions went unanswered, problems were left unsolved, there was no neat conclusion.

Just like reality. Just like life.

By the time I reached the final page, I was full of admiration for the author. Here was not merely a "young writer of great promise" but a great writer, period. Any reservations I had were due solely to my own personal views on what constitutes "a good read" – I suppose I'm a bit conservative in my taste – and consequently all the theorising about "who is really the author/ how much control does he-she have/what is really real" etc. left me a little cold. But those characters . . . I could converse with them. I could befriend them. I could argue with them. And the attractive blonde who appeared on page twenty, well, I could fall in love with her. I really could.

Her name, by the way, was Zoë, and she looked a little like Liana, only taller.

40

'I find it so hard to think of her as "Liana"; she's Angela – always has been. To hear people refer to her by what sounds like my own name is really odd ... sort of dislocating. It's actually quite unpleasant.'

'Unpleasant?' We were walking along Eldon Road; by my calculations, we would be standing outside the last house on the left within five minutes. The idea that Liana might be there, that I could be standing face to face with her in just a few moments, was enough to give me palpitations. I was so nervous, I was grateful for any diversion, and was pleased that Lee was talking.

'Well, perhaps unpleasant isn't the right word; but it is uncomfortable. I mean, *why* did she change her name in the first place? Why did she take my name?'

It was a question I had asked myself many times over the weekend, and I had to concede that there *was* something disturbing about it. 'I can *only* think of her as Liana,' I said, unable to answer Lee's questions. 'Perhaps she just liked the name?'

Lee gave me a rather exasperated look, as if she expected better than inanities from me; it was, in retrospect, quite justifiable, but at the time I could not really concentrate on Lee's concerns. I had my own fears to deal with. An entirely new picture had emerged that day, and I was still trying to come to terms with it.

Since returning to England I had learnt that Liana wasn't Liana, but Angela. She had not studied Fine Art at Kent, did not have a younger brother, did not live at her given address. She had run away from home, had been in trouble at some time in the past eighteen months (that is, had been so desperate for money that she had made contact with her despised family) and had lived – was perhaps still living – in a squat in Wood Green. With a man. A man called Keith, who was not especially popular with a nice Italian Mama who ran a café on Charing Cross Road, but was much respected by a greasy yob with a scarred face who served behind the bar of the seediest pub in North London. It was fairly safe to assume that Keith was a scrounger and a drunk. The rest was still a mystery, and I was no longer sure that I wanted to find a solution. Even as we approached the end of the road, half of me wanted to discover nothing, to find that it had been a wild goose chase, that there was no Liana living at the last house on the left, no Keith, no problems.

I'm not sure if Lee picked up on this – I suspect she was well aware of what was going through my mind, but said nothing. After all, we had set out to find Liana, and it was assumed, implicitly, that we might well discover something unpalatable or difficult. After all, why else hadn't she contacted me? Something had to be wrong. I was suddenly made all the more aware of Richard's telling comments; did I really want to get involved? What if there was something seriously wrong with her? How had Richard put it – what if she's nuts?

'What's the matter? Michael?'

'Huh?'

'Why have you stopped? It's not far now.'

'Stopped?' With some confusion I now realised that Lee was several paces ahead of me. I was, in fact, leaning against a garden wall, trying to steady myself.

'Are you okay? You've gone rather pale.'

I was not, as it happens, feeling particularly well. My brow felt cold and clammy, and there was an unpleasantly hot sensation at the back of my neck. My legs did not feel strong, my stomach was loose, and there was a nauseating buzzing sound in my ears.

'Uh, sorry Lee, I . . . I just . . .' I shrugged my shoulders. 'I think I must be scared.'

Lee walked over to me, put her hands on my shoulders, stared straight into my eyes. 'Do you want to wait here? I'll go and find out what the story is.'

'No, I should come with you.'

'Michael . . . you really don't look up to it. Why don't you just sit down for a moment.' She put her hand to my forehead; it felt soothing. I wanted her to leave her hand there, to caress me for a while, to ease away the feelings of discomfort and fear. I wanted her to save me.

'I'm fine, really. I just need to take a couple of deep breaths.' I took hold of her hand. 'This is really good of you, Lee; you didn't have to get involved. I don't know what I would have done . . .'

'We haven't found her yet . . . look Michael, I don't think . . . I mean . . .' She stared unflinchingly at me. 'Stay here,' she said after a few moments. 'Let me just find out what the situation is; as soon as I know what's going on, I'll come straight back. You don't look fit enough to take a shock right now.'

'Shock? What do you mean?'

Lee sighed. 'Michael, neither of us knows what's going on. I won't be happy to find something terrible behind those doors, but whatever it is, I'll cope with it. I've had to learn to live with the idea of my sister as all but dead these past three years. But you . . . you're still in love with her. Just let me find out what's going on. It may be nothing. Just wait.'

She didn't stop long enough to allow me to argue. I waited by the wall while Lee wandered up to the last house, up the pathway to the front door. There was a shallow porch which meant that, while I could just make out the front door opening, I could not see, from this angle, who had opened it. I watched Lee mouth a few words, then fall silent. She nodded a couple of times, then pointed to me. I felt my stomach turn to liquid, and clutched hold of the wall; who was Lee speaking to? What had she said? Why had she pointed?

Lee raced back down the path and came across to me.

'She's not there,' she said softly.

'Who were you talking to?'

'A young woman called Robyn; one of the squatters.

She knows Angela . . . I mean Liana. I told her we were very worried and she said that we were welcome to come in and chat for a while.'

'Where's Keith?'

'He's not in . . . I didn't ask where he was. Do you feel up to it?'

I nodded. 'Yes, of course.'

'This is Michael.'

'Hi. I'm Robyn,' said the girl, and beckoned us in to the hallway.

'Hello,' I said, rather feebly. 'It's good of you to see us like this.'

'No problem.'

She pushed open a door and ushered us into the front room. When I'd thought of Liana living in a squat, my worst fears had been activated; I imagined all sorts of gruesome scenarios; filth, dirt, rats, people sleeping on floors; no water or electricity; garbage piled up in every corner; damp, musty smells emanating from peeling wallpaper; the stench of rotten cabbage wafting in from the kitchen. The reality was very different. The front room was not only clean and tidy, but comfortable too. It was very simply furnished; two covered mattresses folded into seats, a dozen scatter cushions, a coffee table made from an offcut of chipboard and a couple of orange crates. The floor was covered in a mosaic of carpet remnants which was surprisingly attractive, and from the walls, which had been painted white, hung a couple of brightly coloured posters. A large bow window gave the room a light, airy feeling; even the curtains had a cottagey feel to them, manufactured from some bleached out hessian. Swing doors at the back of the room led to what looked like a small kitchen. Piano music – Debussy, I think – emanated softly from an ageing cassette recorder in the corner, and altogether the atmosphere was very calm and pleasing.

We sat down on the mattresses while Robyn gathered up the mugs and cups on the table.

'Tea or coffee?'

'Whatever's easiest,' said Lee.

Robyn smiled. 'Sure; I'll just put the kettle on,' she said, and wandered into the adjoining room.

'This wasn't what I was expecting at all,' whispered Lee.

'I know; it's quite a revelation. I was expecting Dante's *Inferno*.'

Lee nodded conspiratorially. 'It rather puts my mind at ease; I'd had visions of my sister living in squalor all these years. I wish I'd known she was in a place like this.'

'What exactly did you say to Robyn?'

'I told her the truth; that I was Liana's sister, that I hadn't seen her for a while, that you'd met her in India, and we were worried about her.'

'When was the last time Robyn saw her?'

'She said that Liana was living here up until three months ago. That's all I know.'

Robyn returned with three steaming hot mugs of coffee. 'Hope you drink it black; we're out of milk and sugar,' she said apologetically.

'This is fine, thank you,' I said.

'So, what do you want to know?'

I looked at Lee. Now that we were here, I wasn't sure where to start. I was so worried about what sort of answers might come my way that I was reluctant to ask the questions. Again, Lee must have sensed this, as she took up the conversation easily.

'How long was Liana living here?'

'About two years I think; she actually moved in some time before me, so it's a bit difficult to say. Keith and John were already here, and there was another girl, but she left shortly after I arrived. For most of the time it was just the four of us.'

'And now it's just you, Keith and John?'

'Yeah, although I suspect someone else'll move in soon enough. Can I have one of these?' She pointed to the packet of cigarettes I'd left on the table.

'Of course.'

'Ta. That's another thing we've run out of.'

I lit the cigarette for her while Lee continued with the questions.

'Where's Keith now?'

Robyn raised her eyebrows and gave a rather deliberate little sniff. 'God knows. Getting pissed, probably.'

'Did you know Liana was going to leave?'

Robyn drew heavily on the cigarette, and allowed the smoke to curl slowly out of the side of her mouth, savouring every last wisp. 'The only thing that surprised me was that she waited so long, what with the way Keith used to treat her. To be honest, she should have moved out ages ago.'

This was exactly the sort of thing I didn't want to hear. I grabbed a cigarette and lit up swiftly. I could feel my pulse rate starting to rise, and the first traces of adrenaline beginning to course through me in preparation for fight or flight.

'Did they not get on then?'

'Depends what you call "getting on". They used to argue like fuck, day and night. He really treated her like shit. I mean, none of us had any money, and Liana would do everything she could to bring in a bit extra so we all could eat better. Keith would just take whatever he could and use it to go down the pub and get tanked up. Then he'd come back, completely arseholed, and start abusing the shit out of the rest of us. I wouldn't take his shit, ever, so I'd just ignore him. Liana however used to rise to the bait every time, and like a fool she'd end up making him even more angry. It was asking for trouble.' She took another deep drag on the cigarette. 'He could be pretty violent sometimes.'

'He used to hit her?'

'Oh yeah. He used to rough her up sometimes. We had to get the doctor in once, her lip was bleeding so badly. Keith could be a right bastard.'

'Why did she put up with it?'

'Why else? She was crazy for him. I don't think I've ever seen anyone so devoted to another person. Not that this is a sufficiently good reason to allow yourself to get beaten up every other night, but I guess that's how it goes sometimes. Isn't there that line in *Streetcar Named Desire*, something about the things that go on between a man and a woman . . . are you okay?' Robyn leaned over towards me, touched my forearm.

'I'm fine,' I said, the bile rising in my throat. 'Really . . . it's just a bit upsetting.' Lee reached across and took my hand.

'Do you want to go?'

'No, I'll be okay. Carry on; let's find out all we can.'

'I'm sorry; did I say something . . . ?'

Lee shook her head. 'No, honestly Robyn, we have to know this stuff. Like Michael says, it's just a bit upsetting.'

'Yes, of course . . . I've probably been a bit blunt, made it sound much worse than it really was. You see, the thing was, in his own way, Keith really did care for Liana. They really did seem to be in love. But I guess in the end it just got too much for her. I don't think he ever meant to hurt her; he had his own problems – as we all did – it's just that he used to take it out on her. And you know what they say about these sort of things . . . she must have, well, not wanted it exactly, but it must have met some need in her, or else she'd never have put up with it that long. Oh shit, have I said the wrong thing again?'

I was on my feet and through the front door before Robyn had finished the sentence. I made it as far as the pavement before the suffocating need to throw up brought me to my knees. I was still retching pathetically when I felt Lee's hand on the back of my neck. There was nothing she could have said that would have helped me then. All I could see was a vision of Liana's tortured expression the night she pleaded with me not to hit her, and all I could think was: I am a child, lost in an adult's world too frightening to contemplate. Poor Liana.

Poor me.

41

What are you going to say? That I should have guessed? That I shouldn't have been so upset, that anyone could see it coming? That's easy for you to say, with the benefit of hindsight, with all the relevant details neatly sifted out for you and put out in tidy piles for your inspection. Yes, I know; you could see it coming. Well done. Aren't you the clever one. Well, I'm sorry to say that, as must be evident from my reaction at the time, I was not fully prepared for what I had to listen to. I had my suspicions, certainly; a beautiful woman knows every sexual trick in the book and claims to be a virgin, screams "don't hit me" every time I make love to her, and can down half a bottle of brandy without flinching, yes, yes, yes... *of course* I had my suspicions. But I didn't dare give voice to them. Who wants to hear that sort of stuff? Who wants to believe it? Would you?

I know what we all say; honesty is what we want. We demand it. "Don't lie to me, don't deceive me," we say; "I'd rather hear it from your lips than..." oh for fucksake, what a load of old bollocks. Who wants to hear the truth? I didn't want the truth; I didn't want to hear that Liana had been living with – was in love with – a mad bastard, an alcoholic who beat her up three times a week, that she was, by implication, an alcoholic herself . . . I didn't want that. I wanted the lie, the lie that Liana told me, about her happy childhood and the devoted school friend and the loving parents and the degree and . . . and . . . and . . . *yes*, I wanted to believe I had been the first, of course I did. What would you rather have had, the beautiful lie or the tawdry reality?

There are times when honesty, like reality, is vastly overrated. I'm not even sure where we get this desire for honesty from, especially when you look at the lives we lead. We must spend ninety per cent of our free time indulging in activities that have nothing to do with reality or honesty. When was the last time you went to the movies to see real life, to see an honest portrayal of reality? Is there such a thing? Of course not. I'd bet good money you went to the movies to be entertained, whisked into a fantasy, to escape the reality of your everyday existence. Not a great deal of honesty in that activity if you ask me. Do you enjoy the soaps on TV? Are they honest? Are they real? Are they, hell. Listened to any good songs recently? Is your life like the lyrics? What about the last decent novel you read. What about that sparkling, crackling dialogue? Do people really talk like that? Does it matter? And what would you rather have, an honest word-for-word verbatim slice of everyday life, or a piece of clever fiction, an elegant conceit?

And at night, when you crawl into your dreams, what

would you rather have; a view of life in the living room, or visions of Elysium?

Given our propensity to dwell in the fictitious, it's a wonder we make such a fuss about honesty. Why, exactly, is the truth good while lies are evil? It strikes me that there is nothing reasonable about this piece of moral dogmatism, but I doubt there's a person out walking the earth who believes differently. And yet, there must be some moral ambivalence about this; why else would we have invented the white lie, which is nothing more than a morally sanctioned slice of evil, a justifiable sin. Wonderful things, white lies; a bit like that confection you could buy once upon a time, you know, the one you could eat between meals without ruining your appetite. We accept that there are degrees of lying, but only one order of truth. Lies come in all sizes and colours, from whopping great to teeny weeny, but truths are all the same. This strikes me as discrimination on a grand scale. It's about time that black truths and white lies were accorded equivalent status. Besides, if something is absolute, then its opposite cannot be variable. Hot and cold are merely extremes of a temperature scale, dependent upon localised conditions. One is not exclusively good, the other bad; that would be nonsense. The same applies to up and down, big and small, hard and soft... why not truth and lies? There are as many bad truths as there are good lies, in the same way that there are as likely to be black truths which are morally dubious as there are white lies which may be sanctioned. Which is why we are perfectly happy to allow writers, film directors and politicians to lie to us;

we actually *prefer* the lie to the truth. So, if we have given our law makers and dream makers a mandate to lie to us, why is the same privilege not extended to our families, friends and loved ones? It would be so much easier, so much less stressful. More to the point, it would be a damn sight more consistent. We could all stop pretending. The truth of the matter is, if we hadn't been told otherwise, we would rather they lied to us too. And, I would suggest, that makes it a very black truth indeed.

42

Robyn showed me to the bathroom where I cleaned myself up as best I could, but no matter how many times I rinsed out my mouth, I could not get rid of that terrible taste. Robyn offered us both more coffee, but all I wanted was to get out of the house and away. Lee thanked Robyn for her time, while I apologised once again. Robyn was terribly concerned, and I did my best to assure her that I was all right – just a bit shaken, nothing to worry about – before we left. She promised to contact us as soon as she heard anything.

As we walked back down Eldon Road I considered the new information we had gleaned. Robyn hadn't gone into too many details about how Liana had made enough money for her and Keith to survive on, but the fact that they did indeed survive and that she had also somehow managed to save enough to go to India suggested all manner of illicit activity. And while Robyn did not go so far as to suggest that Liana had been on the game, it remained an open question. One thing was for sure; she must have been saving secretly for some time, and this would account for why she stayed with Keith so long, especially once he started to beat her up. I think it was this information that particularly upset Lee. She blamed herself for not having given her sister more money when she had asked for it. It was left to me to remind her that Liana could have gone home anytime and asked her parents for help, but had chosen not to.

Why I should suddenly have become the fount of reason is beyond me. Perhaps I had found the revelations at the squat so distressing that the only way I could handle them was to assume the wise-old-man position and hope that Lee would be so impressed by my stoicism that she would see my emotional reaction as nothing more than stress or tension and not, as was the case even then, a manifestation of this obsessive mania that was beginning to take over my life.

In such circumstances as these, having been thrust into a nightmare world where nothing is as it appears, I suppose I might have chosen just to throw in the towel. Love may indeed conquer all, but let's face it, by the time I left the squat, any illusions I might have had about a pure, wonderful, loving girl called Liana who loved and adored me had all but disappeared and, more to the point, I was still no closer to finding out where she was. As Richard had said, if she had wanted to see me, she would have contacted me; I was beginning to see why she had not bothered. Back in England, the life she had constructed for my benefit would have been shown up for what it was; a fable. Perhaps it was this knowledge – that inevitably I would find out the truth – that had convinced her to leave India (and me) so suddenly. And not being able to tell me the truth herself, she had left me her old address, knowing full well I would come face to face with her family and by extension the rest of the details of her true life, without her ever having to be a witness to the process. Weighing up all the evidence, the sensible thing would have been to admit defeat then and there, resign myself to the fact that my love affair with Liana was over, go off quietly to grieve the loss, and then get back to living a normal life. That would have been the sensible thing to do. But do not forget, I was not a sensible young man. I was obsessed. More to the point, the mystery of Liana's whereabouts and my desire to find her was the only thing that would enable me to maintain contact with Lee. And if you're thinking to yourself: wait a minute, *who* exactly is he after, then I'm afraid I have to admit that, as Lee and I made our way back to Wood Green underground station, I had about as good an answer to that question as you do.

43

I would not wish to be considered a pessimist but, the fact is, I believe we spend the majority of our lives in a state of deep confusion. This often manifests itself as a sort of continuous comatose condition in which the protagonist does as little thinking as is humanly possible, as this is by far the safest way of getting through the day without getting hurt. Once you start to think, you're letting yourself in for big trouble; it's so easy to find yourself tripping up over a bit of stray morality, an untidy strand of ethics that someone forgot to stash away properly. If you're not looking where you're going, you're almost certain to fall foul of these things, or worse. You may be wandering along one day minding your own business when all of a sudden you stumble into a great gaping question. Not a "Where did I put my wallet" or "Did I remember to feed the cat", question; oh no, I mean a Question; a "Why am I here", Question, or a "What am I doing with my life", Question. You know the ones; sneaky little fuckers that have no right to be fooling around with miserable little half-wits like you and me.

I mean, talk about mismatch, talk about being outnumbered. Poor little dozy human being, up against cosmic conundrums; I mean, it's hardly a fair fight is it?

Mind you, there's no one to blame but yourself; once you start thinking, you're leaving yourself wide open, you're making yourself vulnerable, you are – to coin a phrase – asking for it. Don't come running to me with your nose bloodied because you ran slap bang into a Question, or fell flat on your face because you tripped up over an unseen philosophical principle. I can't do anything about it. You'll just have to suffer it. Like I said; better not to think in the first place; better to just get on with it.

Most importantly, avoid those nasty moral perplexities, as they will get you nowhere. Before you know it, you'll be juggling with absolutes, a priori conditions, and doctrinal catechisms, and you're bound to fuck up somewhere. I can guarantee that if you spend too long doing moral balancing acts you'll fall over; you'll end up being wrong or guilty or both. It's a no-win situation, so you'd be well advised not to play the game in the first place. Unless, of course, you're a masochist, in which case, be my guest.

Take, for example, this interesting little scenario. A man has fallen completely and profoundly in love with a woman who has disappeared from the face of the earth. He is convinced he cannot live without her, and in his efforts to find her he meets and befriends the woman's older sister who, it turns out, is also dead sexy, and before anyone can say, "You sneaky, deceitful, two-timing little hypocrite," he is wondering how he is going to get the older sister into bed.

What? Oh for Christ's sake, you're so busy occupying the moral highground that you probably can't even see what's going on. Stop damning and blasting him for a moment and look at the facts. He's been conned; this supposed dream woman has misled him from the word go, lied to him and abused him. On account of her, he's cut short his trip of a lifetime, been worried sick for three days, and cried himself to sleep. He has been stood up on the grand scale, and you're pointing a finger of reproof and making silly noises with your tongue and front teeth. Come on, give the guy a break. It just so happens that throughout this miserable ordeal, the only kindness he's seen has come from a charming and delightful young lady who, he believes, is showing more than casual interest in him and . . . well, what would you do? Okay, so it's all progressing with what might seem to be indecent haste, but remember, the guy's young, and things *do* happen faster when you're twenty-one. If he starts getting tangled up in the morality and ethics of the situation, he's going to miss one of the all-time great opportunities; if he stops and listens to his peers, he's only going to get confused and upset; if he starts thinking, he's fucked. Better that he sinks into that wonderful deep, unquestioning confusion (see under: Human Condition) and with a bit of luck he may get laid. Come on, you should be encouraging him, shouting from the terraces, waving your scarves, hoping he'll score. After all, we all know that he'll pay for it in the end, so we might as well let him have some fun while he can, a brief moment's pleasure in a lifetime of pain. It's not all that important, after all; he's already made his promises, his commitments. He's struck his bargains with God, and his own conscience and twisted obsessions will ensure that he doesn't renege on that. So how about a bit of support from the back rows there? How about a little cheering as our hero steps centre stage and, in an endearing little monologue, confesses that, whilst he still loves Liana with all his heart, there's this other business which has nothing to do with love and everything to do with hormones, and begging the audience their indulgence, if they wouldn't mind being patient for a short while, he's just going to nip backstage for a quickie. Thank you.

44

We checked into a cheap travellers' hotel near Victoria station, registered as Mr and Mrs Roger Michaels, crept up to the room and, shaking with a mixture of sexual anticipation and something that felt like adulterous guilt but could not technically be so, we went to bed. Before Liana had waltzed into my life, I would never have believed I'd be involved in a situation such as this. What was it that had changed in my life? For years women hadn't given me a second look. Why, suddenly, did beautiful women want to jump into bed with me within a day or two of meeting me? It was Lee who first used the phrase "sexual magnetism" to describe my supposed attraction. However, she was not the last, and if the truth be told, I still don't know what the expression means. Perhaps it was chemical? Perhaps at some time around my twenty-first birthday a couple of glands went critical mass and started overproducing pheromone attractors in such high concentrations that I was, literally, a walking mating machine. Perhaps it was a combination of my voice (which had recently dropped a further half octave), my slight astigmatism which caused me to focus more intently on people (very appealing, people love to be the sole focus of someone's attention), and my obvious, desperate lust for beautiful women. I mean, who can resist someone who wants them that badly? Whatever, here I was again, about to climb into bed with a woman who could make Venus cry, and all I could think to myself was: I hope Liana doesn't find out about this. Not, "Oh God, this is terribly wrong, immoral, unethical and a really shitty thing to do . . ."; not, "How can I be so fickle, I was crying over Liana just three hours ago for fucksake!"; nor even, "What are the implications of what I am doing regarding the relationship between these two sisters?". Oh no, I was thinking, "I hope Liana doesn't find out," and it wasn't because I thought she'd be hurt, but because I couldn't help but believe by this stage that Liana was, by all accounts, extremely unstable and it was just possible that, should she discover that I was humping her sister, she might just kill me.

It was, of course, the risk, the implicit danger that acted as such a tremendous aphrodisiac. No sooner had the bedroom door slammed shut behind us than we were ripping off each other's clothes with such ferocious intention that one might have thought the end of the world were nigh.

Lee's appetite for sex was of the same order as her younger sister's, and her approach quite similar, but there was one difference which, bearing in mind the location of our illicit tryst, could have caused a few problems. Lee was a good deal more vocal in her – how should I put it – response. She was also rather more specific in her use of language, which was both graphic and perfectly enunciated. I think the whole of South West London was a party to her directive that I, "Fuck harder, harder, harder you miserable prick, fuck me like you mean it!", although frankly, at the time, I couldn't have cared less.

She was lovely, of course, and I particularly liked her playful manner and her insistence that there was no point paying out good money for a hotel if we wanted to sleep, so we might as well make good use of the facilities. Had she suggested we camp out in the park for a week I would probably have agreed. This was my first experience of illicit sex; I really did feel as if I had just embarked on an affair, and rather than feel guilty, I was exhilarated. Even as dawn broke I still had no idea whether this was merely an elevated one-night-stand or the start of something rather more substantial. After all the emotional traumas of the previous few days, making love with Lee was like an antidote to the confusion and heartbreak. For a few hours that night I was able to seek perfect solace in the arms of another woman, a woman who was both a complete stranger and also, by virtue of her closeness to Liana, like an old friend. And despite the rather furtive nature of our liaison, it felt neither dishonourable nor tawdry; if anything, there was a rather ingenuous air to our activities, like a couple of kids who have been left unsupervised for the first time and are discovering just how much fun it is to play when no one's watching.

In the morning, just prior to leaving the hotel, it was Lee who said what had, until then, been left unspoken.

'She must never know, Michael. If she comes back, if you ever see her again, you must never tell her about this. You understand, don't you?'

I nodded. In fact, I did not at that time understand very much of anything, which just goes to show how naïve I was. But Lee was much more astute than me. Not that it would make any difference; it was already too late for that.

I saw Lee almost every day that week. Her parents were away on holiday for a fortnight, but we spent very little time at the house. Instead, we would meet at the café in Charing Cross Road, where Lee continued to taunt the Italian boys, especially Tony, who was quite puzzled by her behaviour. The café held an important association for us, and became, in some ways, the centre of our liaison, around which everything else revolved. We did all the things that lovers do when they first meet; we went to the cinema to see a romantic film, to the theatre to laugh loudly at the latest Ayckbourn comedy, and to a rather nice Malaysian restaurant (which neither of us could afford) where, apart from eating too much, we also managed to get very silly on two bottles of over-priced Sauvignon. It was a great week.

My parents did not know what was going on, but were delighted to see my spirits restored. Richard, who was delighted to see me behaving so despicably, even offered his bedsit for one night, but we declined, preferring instead to return either to Lee's parent's house in

Godalming, or more often, to the nasty little hotel around the back of Victoria station. It was more in keeping with the tenor of our relationship; we were having an affair, and affairs were carried out in seedy hotels in drab parts of London. Everyone knew that.

We didn't mention Liana, love, or what would happen if. We didn't ask, "What does this mean?" or, "What are we doing?"

And we didn't say anything at all when, a week later, as we made love on Lee's parents' living room floor, a brick crashed through the front window pane, showering us with a thousand shards of glass.

45

Do you think it meant that I did not love Liana, that it was all make believe? Do you think I cared less about her because I was screwing her sister? Is that how life works? What was it Richard had said about fidelity? Perhaps Richard's reasoning was merely to justify his selfish behaviour, but he did have a point; there may be reasons why infidelity is wrong, but they have nothing to do with the sort of superficial morality that is usually waved about with such high-minded superiority. I was enjoying being with Lee; I was enjoying her company, the access I had to her lovely body, her warmth and the excitement we generated in bed together. But I did not love Lee; I was not in love with her, and there was no way I could fall in love with her. There was a completely different feel to our relationship; it was fun, yes, and we did get up to some pretty erotic tricks which necessitated a greater intimacy than one would have thought appropriate for what was little more than a casual fling. But let's face it, that was all it was: a fling. There was a spark, a flash of electricity; there was mutual need and equally mutual understanding. Should the circumstances of our meeting have really made a difference? Just supposing I had never met Liana; suppose I had bumped into Lee at a party and we had hit it off and gone to bed together with the same casual intention that locked us together then? No one would have raised an eyebrow. If we had continued to meet in seedy hotels, no one would have minded. If we had sneaked a night or two together at her parents's house whilst they were out of the country, no one would have objected.

Unfortunately, the circumstances of our meeting were not as simple as that, and someone *did* object, and made the objection known by hurling a brick through the window, a brick which, whilst having no identifying marks, made the same accusation that you're all making now.

"How could you?"

It's an interesting question. It deserves an answer. Ideally, the answer would placate the enquirer in such a way that the incident need never be mentioned again. Alas, no such answer exists. You may wish to choose an answer for yourself that offers a neat explanation. How about, "Because he's an evil, thoughtless bastard." Or, "Because he has no scruples, no moral sense, no soul." Or how about, "Because he doesn't know better," or, "Because he's a victim of social conditioning," or, "Because he's a slave to his hormones," or, "Because he's young and wants to experiment." Let's face it, even if all the above were true, would it have vindicated me in your eyes? Would you have said "fair enough" and forgiven me? I doubt it. More to the point, would any or all of the possible reasons or excuses have vindicated me in the eyes of a woman who felt she had been in her sister's shadow all her life, a woman who had been physically beaten, emotionally abused and sexually manipulated, perhaps by a succession of men, culminating in an alcoholic misfit who particularly liked slapping her about after they'd made love? Would any excuse or reason suffice for a woman who, within a matter of years, would no longer know her own identity, no longer recognise her face in the mirror, be unable to differentiate between the true facts of her personal history and a mythical version that she had unwittingly manufactured to protect herself?

Would any of it have made any difference to a madwoman?

Richard may have been right about fidelity; he may even have been right about love. But I'm afraid he was much mistaken about guilt. Guilt has nothing to do with feeling insecure. Richard may have enjoyed *Crime and Punishment*, but he certainly didn't understand it. We may do all manner of extraordinary things because of love, but they are nothing compared to the things we will do because of guilt.

However, when you combine an excess of both love and guilt, only then will you see someone behave in ways that defy all reason. Especially if that someone happens to be an obsessive neurotic . . .

46

I pulled on my jeans as swiftly as I could, taking care not to step on the jagged glass, and ran to the front door.

'What are you doing? Are you mad?'

'Just stay there; make sure you don't cut yourself . . .'

'Michael!'

I opened the door and peered out into the darkness. I could hear my pulse throbbing in my temples, distracting me, tugging at my attention. My right hand was bleeding – just a scratch, I could feel nothing. The air was bitterly cold, and everything was so still, so quiet, that at first I didn't even notice her. Then I heard the quiet sobbing noises that I'd become so familiar with.

She was kneeling on the lawn, her face in her hands. I knew it was her; even in the half-light she was instantly recognisable; the silhouette of her body, her posture, the gentle heaving of those lovely shoulders.

A million thoughts rushed forward, each jostling and elbowing to make room for themselves, each demanding recognition, requesting attention. For every thought there was an accompanying emotion, and wedged in between were a number of physical responses which were mostly irregularities of pulse and breath. I had no sooner set eyes upon her than I was a mess of confused responses, unable to speak or act.

I stood there for a moment or two, waiting for a sense of normality to return, hoping something would happen so that I wouldn't have to make a decision. As it happened, no sooner had the thought entered my head than Lee appeared and with a half-whispered "Angela", pushed past me and ran on to the lawn where she threw her arms around her totally unresponsive sister.

There have been many moments in my life when I have wished not to exist, when the sheer effort of living was just too great, the problems too harsh, the reasons "for" mere shadows when placed alongside the reasons "against". It is not a suicidal wish; I have never wanted to die; just to be for ever unconscious, no longer aware of my own existence. As I watched Lee hug her sister close and rock her gently, as Liana's sobs seeped into the cold winter's night, I was overcome with such a feeling. I did not want to be there, standing on the doorstep of a suburban detached in Surrey watching this latest bizarre scenario; I did not want to be anywhere. I did not want to be. It didn't make sense. In theory, I should have been overjoyed. Liana was back, she was here, she had returned; we could start again. I should have been delighted, but I was not. I was terrified.

What was it I sensed that cold December night? In those few moments that followed, did I actually feel my freedom disappear, leaching into the air, the soil, the ether? Did I really see my life strung out ahead of me like a reel of film, predestined, a life over which I would no longer have control? Did I know, in that moment, that the door that had threatened to slam shut had already done so, that the key had been turned in the lock and thrown away?

It cannot have been more than a minute later when Lee looked up at me and called.

'Michael!' There was a desperation in her voice that I had never heard before; I knew something was terribly wrong, that I would have to take responsibility, that I would be asked to act.

I walked over slowly, trying to regain my breath, to steady my nerves. Lee's eyes remained on me the whole time.

'There's something wrong, Michael; I don't think she knows who I am.'

'What?' I knelt down in front of the two sisters. Liana was staring straight ahead, focusing on empty space. She had stopped crying. Her face was almost completely devoid of emotion; she looked like a shop-window dummy. 'Liana?' I took her hand; she was cold to the touch, lifeless. I squeezed her hand but she did not respond. 'Liana? Are you okay? Liana?' Nothing.

'What's wrong? Michael?'

'I don't know,' I croaked. Once again, my world was falling apart. There was something wrong with her, something desperately wrong with Liana. If previously she had been fragile, on the edge, then now she had fallen and finally cracked.

And it was all my fault.

'Let's get her inside.' I looked at Lee and for a moment the enormity of it all flooded over me. She must have seen it in my eyes, because she looked away. My life with Lee was over; my life with Liana was just about to begin. My God was keeping me to my word; I had touched the stars, I had inhaled heaven's breath, I had known ecstasy, and now it was my turn to pay.

Even in the poor light, with her eyes and cheeks red from crying and the sad, blank expression in her face, she was still as beautiful as ever. This was what I had begged God for; to be with this woman. In so doing, I had forfeited my right to a happy future. This was where it all ended. This was where it all began.

'Liana, we're going inside now. Come on.' We helped her to her feet and guided her to the house. She said nothing, allowing herself to be led like a lost, lonely child.

47

It is all something of a blur now. I cannot recall exactly what happened. We called a doctor, I think, who said something about shock and mild catatonia, and suggested we put her to bed, keep her warm and call if there were any problems. For two days Liana said nothing. We fed her, kept her warm, never left her alone, not for a moment. Lee and I said little to each other; she wondered whether she should try to contact her parents, but I advised against it. There was nothing they could do, and anyway, if Liana was in shock, their arrival might only complicate matters. Besides, hadn't they given up on her?

We never did find out how long Liana had been following us, or where she had stayed, or why she had waited so long to confront us. The reason for her disappearance would never come to light. When she finally "came to", she had no recollection of what had happened. The period between when she had arrived back in London and "woken up" in her old bedroom was a complete blank. She was still a little dazed, and remained so for a few days. Her memory seemed haphazard and unreliable, an amalgam of real events and totally contrived episodes; she could remember India, but not what she had been doing in the preceding months. She knew she hadn't seen Lee for a while, but thought it closer to six months than eighteen. It was not until much later that I discovered how advanced this mythomania was. At the time, I didn't really care. Liana had indeed returned, and she was so pleased to see me, so enthusiastic, that for a moment I genuinely thought that everything would be okay.

Her parents were due back from their holiday by then, and we all thought it sensible that Liana be somewhere else when they returned. Mum and Dad offered to put her up, but this didn't feel terribly comfortable. It was Richard who came to the rescue, and this time I did take him up on his offer to move in. Richard went to stay with Mandy or Melanie or whoever it was he was busy with, and Liana and I moved into his bedsit. But it was not for long. A week later I got my first job working as a journalist on a local newspaper. We rented a tiny flat near Highbury Corner. Liana took a part-time job in a fashionable clothes shop in the West End, and within a month we were settled and, much to our joint delight, happy. It was all far too good to be true. Work was fun, the flat, though small, located in a great area, and we seemed to want for nothing. Every night we would make passionate, death-defying love, and at the weekend we'd retire to bed with nothing but a few packets of cigarettes and a bottle of champagne. It was a return to the magic of those first days together. But it was not to last.

A year later, we were married in the local Registry Office; Mum and Dad, Richard, Lee and Tony (from the café in Charing Cross Road) attended. Liana's parents did not attend. They had never forgiven Liana for the agony she had put them through. They had had nothing to do with her since her return to the fold, and were not about to start just because she was getting married. It seemed impossibly heartless to me, and I even took the liberty of writing to them, but I never received a reply. Lee said she could do nothing to persuade them, so that was that.

Three months after the wedding, Liana had her first major breakdown, more severe than anything I had seen so far. That was when we sought professional help.

Today is our last day together for six months. Liana is not speaking to me; she ranted and raved all night, and is now so exhausted that she has neither the energy nor the inclination to converse. Tomorrow I will drive her down to Devon, to leave her in the capable hands of Doctor Jerome and his merry band of helpers. The following day I will fly to Jakarta and start the six-month odyssey that will, hopefully, provide me with enough material to keep us both alive for another year.

If I have given the impression that I resent this, any of this, then forgive me. In case you are in any doubt, understand that I do these things not because I have to, but because I want to. If I was paid at higher rates, then I would work for just three months, and I would take Liana and look after her for nine months of the year.

You see, she may be crazy, she may spend half her time hating me, or wanting to kill me, but Liana is still the most enchanting, the most desirable, the most beautiful woman I have ever known. And I love her.

Desperately.